KU-409-768

AFTER THE STORM

With the war over and Matthew back home with her, Tessa is looking forward to starting their married life together. But Matthew seems unable to settle to civilian life. He lies to Tessa that he is seeking work when in truth he is meeting another woman. Who is the mysterious Iris Phelps? And what does she know about Matthew that he feels unable to share with Tessa? Is their marriage over before it has really begun?

SALLY HAWKER

—————— ◆ ——————

AFTER THE STORM

Complete and Unabridged

LINFORD
Leicester

First published in Great Britain in 2012

First Linford Edition
published 2021

Copyright © 2012 by DC Thomson & Co. Ltd.,
and Sally Hawker
All rights reserved

A catalogue record for this book is available
from the British Library.

ISBN 978–1–4448–4721–5

Published by
Ulverscroft Limited
Anstey, Leicestershire

Printed and bound in Great Britain by
TJ Books Ltd., Padstow, Cornwall

This book is printed on acid-free paper

KENT
ARTS & LIBRARIES

DV

12/21
Doreen S.
MRS TURTIE
29.8.23

Books should be returned or renewed by the last
date above. Renew by phone **03000 41 31 31** or
online *www.kent.gov.uk/libs*

Libraries Registration & Archives

CUSTOMER
SERVICE
EXCELLENCE

CSE

Kent
County
Council
kent.gov.uk

C161059692

SPECIAL MESSAGE TO READERS
THE ULVERSCROFT FOUNDATION
(registered UK charity number 264873)
was established in 1972 to provide funds for
research, diagnosis and treatment of eye diseases.
Examples of major projects funded by the
Ulverscroft Foundation are:-

- The Children's Eye Unit at Moorfelds Eye Hospital, London
- The Ulverscroft Children's Eye Unit at Great Ormond Street Hospital for Sick Children
- Funding research into eye diseases and treatment at the Department of Ophthalmology, University of Leicester
- The Ulverscroft Vision Research Group, Institute of Child Health
- Twin operating theatres at the Western Ophthalmic Hospital, London
- The Chair of Ophthalmology at the Royal Australian College of Ophthalmologists

You can help further the work of the Foundation
by making a donation or leaving a legacy. Every
contribution is gratefully received. If you would
like to help support the Foundation or require
further information, please contact:

THE ULVERSCROFT FOUNDATION
The Green, Bradgate Road, Anstey
Leicester LE7 7FU, England
Tel: (0116) 236 4325
website: www.ulverscroft-foundation.org.uk

April 30, 1945

Once beyond the gates of Ambrose's military clothing factory, Tessa Lane paused to button her mother's grey woollen coat around her shoulders before she set off at a brisk pace towards the grocer's shop on Moseley Road.

With any luck she'd make it there before old Vince Watkins turned the sign and locked the door. Trading hours at the shop were dependent upon how many folk Vince clocked coming down the road on his six o'clock sojourn from behind the counter, but the mass exodus from Birmingham's factories at six on the dot usually ensured a fair few women armed with their ration books.

A little way ahead of Tessa hurried three or four women who worked alongside her at Ambrose's, hunched over sewing-machines ten hours a day as they churned out service dress tunics, skirts and trousers. Watching them disappear down the narrow ginnel that was a short-cut to Moseley Road, Tessa quickened her pace. Her weekly rations she'd pick up tomorrow if it saved a long wait in the queue, but she'd promised Anne some sweets for her birthday and she'd no intention of returning to Hockley Street without them.

A Brummie lass born and bred, Tessa knew the city and its secrets as she knew the palm of her hand; a quick detour between terraces and she'd only to pick her way across a wasteland that had once been a housing plot to find herself in Moseley Road.

So intent was she on buying Anne's dolly mixtures before Vince Watkins shut up shop, she barely glanced at the debris of war, the houses that had stood firm against the onslaught but were little more than shells, long since cleared of salvaged treasures and no doubt looted of anything that remained, their window-frames blasted free of splintered glass to become dark holes, staring blankly across a road of bomb sites and boarded-up shop fronts.

When the bombs had been dropped back in 1940, Moseley Road had copped a bit of a pasting, but Vince Watkins had been one of the lucky ones: aside from half-a-dozen tiles off the roof and a bit of smoke damage, the shop had emerged unscathed.

By a twist of fate Tessa, too, had come through it unharmed. On that night when they'd seen the worst of it, the most inconvenience she'd faced was a mad scramble to the nearest shelter, while across town her sister-in-law and mother-in-law, the only family she had in Birmingham, had been killed when their house was flattened — the house in which Tessa had lived until that fateful night, the house in which she should have been a sitting target. She should have lost her life along with them, but she'd survived.

If talk could be heeded, the war in Europe had all but run its course.

News reports had settled down because there were fewer attacks to report, and across the country folk in their droves were buying flags and bunting in eager anticipation of the moment when victory would be declared.

After talking it over with Lillian Cooper, her friend and business partner, Tessa had ordered a bulk supply of ribbons in patriotic colours. At fourpence ha'penny a yard it was a costly investment, but one she hoped to recoup ten times over. Hair bows, rosettes and beribboned handkerchiefs would be relatively simple to produce, and not so expensive that their usual contingent of customers, struggling to spare so much as a penny, could not purchase a little something.

For those with more to spend, Tessa was devoting every spare moment she had to sewing scarves of red, white and blue which she would sell at six shillings a time. Trade at Li'l Tessa's had slowed since clothes had been rationed at sixty-six coupons a year, but with any luck a boom in 'victory' sales might put them firmly back in business.

4

As it had since childhood, her knowledge of every hidden twist and turn of the city served her well. A good few paces ahead of the other women Tessa arrived at the grocer's shop to find, much to her relief, the shutters still up and the sign not yet turned.

But it was not Vince Watkins's usual saunter outside to scour the road for last-minute custom that had ensured his shop remained open. By the looks of it he had yet to venture out from behind the counter, so absorbed was he in listening to the wireless he'd lifted on to it, his ear pressed up close to the speaker as if he was afraid of missing something.

Whatever it was, Tessa had arrived too late to catch it — the melodious harmonies of the Andrews Sisters filled the air as she approached the counter, the unease heavy in her chest the way it always was when there was any news of the war.

But Vince Watkins's face was a picture of triumph as he beamed at her, so keen to tell what he'd just heard that he'd no

5

time to bother with the usual civilities.

'You've heard the news, have you? Old Hitler's dead — dead as a doornail! Chap on the six o'clock bulletin just said it clear as crystal.' He shook his head, bewildered. 'Be a matter o' days now, I reckon, before we're all dancing in the streets. What can I get you, Mrs Lane?'

Tessa found her voice.

'Two ounces of dolly mixtures, please.'

'For young Anne, is it?'

'A birthday treat — she's four today.'

'Is she now? Then she'll have a bit extra and nowt said about it,' Vince declared cheerfully as he measured out the sweets. 'I'm in no mood to penny pinch with the end o' this war just round the corner.'

'You really think it'll be over soon?' To Tessa's own ears her voice sounded quiet. Clearing her throat, she tried again. 'Did they say that on the news?'

'Not in so many words,' Vince admitted, tipping Anne's sweets into a bag and twisting the ends shut. 'Don't take a genius, though.' He waved a dismissive hand across Tessa's attempt to pay him for the extra sweets. 'Put your money away, Mrs Lane. That husband o' yours flying out, is he?' So many times over the past six years she'd been asked about Matthew, how he was, if he was back flying sorties or still on the ground training them young recruits, she almost had it perfected, a fine art. How to answer politely with no sign of how her heart ached with every moment they were kept apart.

'He's been back on active service since the rocket bombs last summer,' she said matter-of-factly, and Vince nodded.

'All hands on deck after that. Especially when they're a natural at flying them Spits like your Matthew is. Not be long now, though, eh? He'll be home before you know it.'

'I hope so,' Tessa said softly.

Six years this summer it would be, six long years since she and Matthew had snatched an hour to dash to the registry office and make their vows before he'd been back driving the afternoon shift on the Selly Oak bus route and she'd rushed back to her machine at Ambrose's to make up the time she'd missed, the thin gold band on her finger the only sign that anything had changed.

He'd been her best friend since childhood. After her mother had died, dropping her upon the mercy of old Esme Lane next door, she and Matthew had grown up together. Not one day had they spent apart; even when he'd gone off to drive buses and she'd been ensconced behind a sewing-machine, never had the sun gone down without them having talked at least once.

If Matthew had been on the day shift, of an evening he and Tessa would make a cup of tea and sit on the back doorstep, side by side, talking and watching the stars. Sometimes they'd not even talk — there'd be no need for words. Matthew's company she treasured above all others. She'd not wanted him to join the RAF, but he'd been determined to enlist. A matter of days after their wedding she'd stood on the platform at New Street Station and watched him disappear.

With no Matthew by her side it had been six very long years. Any leave he'd got had been short and infrequent. For a while he'd been retired from active service to train new recruits on a base in Wales; just a short train journey for Tessa, but had it been three times as long she'd have made it and not grumbled; but now he was back in the air night after night, flying bomber missions out to the Far East, and once more she was constantly terrified that she might lose him.

Turning into Hockley Street, Tessa quickened her pace. If last year's palaver was anything to go by, the place would be crammed to the rafters by now. Bertie's doing, of course. With him playing the piano to a packed crowd in the Black Horse every Saturday afternoon, the whole of Brum would have heard about Anne Cooper's fourth birthday. To any youngsters not despatched to the country long since Bertie had issued an open invitation to his daughter's party.

'It'll be you keeping them entertained then,' Lil had told him in no uncertain terms. 'Daft as a brush, you are. Might want to buy us a bigger house next time you go and invite every child for miles around.'

'Stop fretting,' Bertie had chided his wife fondly. 'Not every day our babby turns four now, is it? She deserves a bit of a fuss made of her.'

'Before she has to share the limelight with the next one, you mean?' Lil had answered darkly, her voice lowered so the words went no further than Bertie's retreating back.

With just a week to go before her second child was due, Lil had bloomed as big as a house. A slightly built, petite woman to begin with, she'd shown from day one that she was expecting Anne, but this next baby looked as if it might be born twice the weight of its big sister.

'They've no need to bother with them barrage balloons here,' Lil had grumbled on catching her reflection in the shop's full-length mirror. 'Might as well just tie ropes to my ankles and float me over the city instead.' Her mood wouldn't be helped any by having to sidestep dozens of little party guests. The sooner Tessa rolled up her sleeves and got stuck in the better.

Unlike Vince Watkins's grocery shop, Li'l Tessa's had closed its doors long since. Five o'clock at the latest Lil would have turned the sign. With her daughter's party to see to she'd be in no mind to dilly-dally on the off-chance of seeing a straggling customer, but in truth there was too little business through the door these days to warrant late opening hours.

Rummaging in her bag for her keys, Tessa let herself into the dimly lit hallway between the shop and the small downstairs kitchen. Excited chatter floated down the stairs and a herd of little footsteps drummed a rhythm above her head as she hung her coat on its hook.

A three-floored town house, number 27, Hockley Street was both home and business. The shop was on the ground floor, Lil and Bertie lived above it and a second flight of stairs led to Tessa's quarters.

But for now she went only as far as the first floor, where she suppressed a smile to see Bertie leading his daughter and about a dozen others in an animated dance around the living-room.

'All them years working for the gas board and a talent like this under his hat.' Dorrie Cooper appeared at Tessa's side. 'I told him, he wants to set himself up as a kiddies' entertainer, make a bit extra. Now's the time to do it, what with the party mood brewing.' She glanced at Tessa. 'Did you hear the news? Well, then, I reckon we're down to counting the days.'

Leaving Dorrie to hand out drinks, Tessa slipped away to the kitchen, in search of Lil. She found her standing over the table, slicing a cucumber.

'Three and six for half a cucumber.' Lil sighed. 'And most of it'll end up trodden into the carpet.' She paused a minute, straightening to rest a hand on the small of her back. 'It's all barmy, Tess. Our Anne would be happy with half the fuss.'

'You know how Bertie likes to entertain,' Tessa reasoned. 'I think you've to expect Dorrie to go overboard for a bit, after you took her in without grumbling.'

'She's Bertie's mother,' Lil pointed out. 'I could hardly see her homeless, nice as it was to be out of that cramped flat of hers and living on our own.'

'She's lucky she weren't in it,' Tessa said flatly. 'It's like a ghost town the other side of Moseley Road. All boarded up or flattened to the ground.'

Taking a knife from the drawer, she began to carve thin slices of bread.

'Take the weight off your feet, Lil. I'll finish up.'

Gratefully, Lil sank into a chair.

'Ta, Tess. There's just the sandwiches to make up, and the cake to slice.'

'And a pot of tea to brew,' Tessa added, lighting the gas under the kettle.

'I'll not say no.' Picking up the 'Birmingham Post' that lay folded on the table, Lil fanned herself with it. 'Old Ambrose will have you all going back to stitching silks soon enough, will he?

Word on the street seems to be this war's near enough done and dusted.'

'That's as maybe, but while there's still battles being fought, there's still tunics want stitching,' Tessa said quietly, spreading a scrape of butter on to thin slices of bread. 'It's not over 'til we've word in black and white.'

Lil nodded sympathetically.

'Been a while since you last heard from Matthew, hasn't it? He'll be flying out night after night, I expect. No time to put pen to paper.'

'Censor's blue pencil blots out half of it anyway.' Tessa sighed.

After six long years of being forced to edit every sentence in case it fell into the wrong hands, she and Matthew had still not grown accustomed to being unable to share every moment of their lives with each other.

'You know he loves you,' Lil pointed out. 'They can't censor that, Tess.'

'I just want to know he's safe,' Tessa murmured. 'All those nights I've lain awake feeling like I can't breathe properly, like I never will, until he's back here safe and sound. I've had enough of it, Lil. I just want him home.'

She'd not meant to say that. Today, Anne's birthday, was a joyous occasion, a chance for them all to forget about the war for five minutes, and for Lil in particular to have a reason to be cheerful before her growing despair at how bloated she looked and how uncomfortable she felt threatened to consume her once more.

Today Tessa's job was to be there for her friend, to make sandwiches and to slice cake, to join in with party games when Lil's heavy frame supported her no further than a spectator's spot in the armchair.

Now was not the time to give way to her own fears.

Lil cradled her cup in her hands, blowing on the steam.

'He'll be home soon enough,' she said matter-of-factly. 'He's made it this far. Then you'll be happy as Larry, the pair of you. Be like a second honeymoon,

15

won't it?' With a sigh she dragged a hand through her once-sleek pageboy-style bob that now hung limply past her shoulders. 'Make the most of it while you can. You'll end up like me before you know it. Be too late then.'

Tessa could feel herself frowning as she rummaged in the cupboard for a clean cloth to cover the sandwiches.

She knew well enough how troublesome Lil had found her second pregnancy, and how desperately she longed for it to end, but once it did she would be further blessed with the family she'd always wanted.

Was she daring to bemoan her lot in life when, compared to Tessa, she had the world and more?

'Bertie loves the bones of you,' Tessa remarked stiffly, addressing her admonishment to the plate of sandwiches. 'Your Anne's a treasure and you'll have a new little one to love any day now. You've the family you came to Birmingham to find, and what's more, you can see for yourself they're safe and well whenever you've a need.'

'So I should count my blessings,' Lil concluded. 'I've not had to suffer the endless drag of waiting and worrying that blights your life, so I've no right to grumble.' She sighed raggedly, her tone a little less blunt as she continued. 'Granted, I don't know the same pain you know, but believe me, Tess, I've no need of a husband off fighting a war to miss what I once had.'

Reaching for the teapot, Tessa lifted the cosy and replenished first Lil's cup then her own. It would do no good to show how hurt she felt that Matthew's absence could possibly be compared to Lil's former life, her pre-childbearing days, when she wore silks and furs and painted her face to look every inch the West End starlet as she belted out popular songs to the accompaniment of Bertie's piano.

'How long's it been since you last went down to the Black Horse of a Saturday afternoon?' she ventured. 'Work wonders for you; that would, Lil. You've got me or

Dorrie on hand to watch the children.'

But Lil shook her head resolutely.

'No time for all that now, have I? All very well singing my heart out when there's none but me and Bertie to think of, but I'm a mother now, I've no business flouncing around the place like a film star.'

'Don't have to stop you singing,' Tessa countered. 'As for being all dolled up, you could shuffle down Gerard Street in your housecoat and you know very well none of them would mind the second you opened your mouth.'

Years of sitting up 'til all hours sewing and mending and she'd developed as sharp an eye as a hawk. The fond smile that passed over Lil's face was fleeting but Tessa caught it all the same.

'Perhaps yon should think about going with Bertie like you used to,' she suggested. 'Even if you don't promise every Saturday, you could set aside one or two a month, Lil. Do you the world of good to be singing again.'

But she'd said too much, she'd pushed

her too far. Lil's face was like stone once more as she lifted a knife to begin slicing Anne's birthday cake.

'I'm done with all that, Tess.'

'Wait.' Tessa's hand on Lil's arm was in time to stop the cake being cut into. 'All right, Lillian Cooper, you can deny the regulars at the Black Horse, but for your own daughter I'm sure you can manage a short ditty.'

'Anne won't give two hoots if she's sung to or not,' Lil stated. 'With Daddy doing a grand job of keeping the troops entertained, and Granny on hand to dish out lemonade, Mummy's obsolete. She'll not notice if I'm stuck here in this chair for the duration.'

'Don't be daft.' Tessa drained the dregs of her tea before getting to her feet. 'I'll carry the cake through, shall I?'

'In case an extra few pounds weight will finish me?' With obvious reluctance, Lil pulled herself up. 'Have it your way, then: You lug the cake and I'll whip up a rousing chorus of 'Happy Birthday' and may we all be happy and jolly as if all it takes is a bit of sugar and a sing-song.'

'I know how uncomfortable you are, Lil,' Tessa ventured quietly as she carefully lifted the cake plate, but the expression Lil fixed her with was cold.

'No offence, Tess, but you have no idea. The day you're hobbling around the place, fit to burst with your first child, only then will you honestly know how uncomfortable I am.' Tessa nodded, averting her eyes to stare fixedly at the crumbs littering Lil's immaculately scrubbed kitchen table. 'You're right,' she murmured. 'What would I know about it? I'm childless. These years you and Bertie have been starting your own little family, I've been waiting for my marriage to start proper, never mind anything else.' She swallowed the lump in her throat. 'I know what it's like to wait, Lil, if I know nothing else.'

Second nature it was to her now, this endless, interminable waiting.

Day after day, toiling over her sewing-machine at Ambrose's, working ten to the dozen to keep her mind off Matthew.

Her feet flying over the pedals on the old Singer, her hands guiding the material as if by instinct, and her thoughts drifting to settle on Matthew, that feeling of comfort tempered now by a hollow loneliness that made her feel as empty as a shell.

She'd been panicking just lately, and it was irrational but she couldn't help it. What if she stopped remembering his face? What if she closed her eyes one day and the image was blurry? She knew it was barmy to think like that. Every precious detail was etched on to her heart. How could she possibly forget him?

On her dressing table she had a photograph of them, taken back in the summer of 1940 at Lil and Bertie's wedding. Matthew had been granted a forty-eight-hour pass so he could come back and be Bertie's best man. Suited and booted in his blue-grey pilot's uniform with the distinctive crest of wings on the tunic, he'd looked so smart and proud.

Tessa was proud of him, too. He'd flown so many defence missions his uniform now bore the green, black and orange medal ribbons awarded for defending his country and he'd been promoted, first to Flight Lieutenant and then Commanding Officer of his squadron down in High Wycombe.

'He's a hero, your Matthew,' the likes of Dorrie and Bertie, and anyone else who fancied adding their twopence worth, were fond of telling her. As if she needed to be told. Not that she'd confess it to any of them, least of all Matthew himself, but sometimes she wished he'd not been so brave, so determined to enlist and do his bit, that he'd trained to do something far less glamorous, if it meant she could have kept him home and safe.

He'd be home soon enough if the war really was on its last legs. But what would he be returning to? Would his old job driving buses around Birmingham still be open to him? Would he be content to live with Tessa in a house in which they were essentially lodgers?

Business at Li'l Tessa's had slowed considerably. Wartime economy was such that women had little to spare for such luxuries as blouses and frocks. At this rate she'd still be scrimping every penny when she was old and grey and no longer fussed where she lived.

She wanted Matthew to have a proper home to come back to, not just a floor of Lil and Bertie's house. The house he and Tessa had grown up in was gone, destroyed in the blitz of 1940, his mother and sister perished, and years of belongings lost for ever. The life Matthew had once known was reduced to rubble.

The one he knew now was a world away. Commanding the skies, manoeuvring his plane in and out of danger with the lightest touch, returning to base undefeated — in this life Matthew soared.

Would he be satisfied to come back down to earth and resume a far more mundane occupation of driving buses around a war-torn city? Would it even matter to Matthew if they saved enough to move into their own house?

'That's the last of them packed off home,' Bertie announced, lowering himself into an armchair with a sigh of relief. 'Far too old for this caper, I am.'

Not yet thirty and ready for the scrap heap.' Tessa grinned at him. 'Give over, Bertie. You've more energy than the rest of us put together.'

'You do your fair share, Tess,' Bertie pointed out, leaning over to unlace his shoes. 'Are you off down the town hall tonight?'

She nodded,

'Clothing drive won't run itself. Mind you, it's hardly worth mending the dish-rags we get landed with these days.'

'Folk have made do and mended 'til there's hardly a stitch left, that's why,' Dorrie reasoned, setting down a tray of teacups on to the table. 'Here, gel, you're not flitting off without a cuppa to warm your bones. Where's our Anne?'

'Putting Mary to bed,' Tessa said, with a smile. 'Lives the life of a princess, that doll does.'

'You're one to talk,' Bertie chided her. 'Who was it knitted Mary her own party dress?'

'I gave her life,' Tessa retorted. 'Only right I should clothe her. Besides, who made Mary her own little crib?'

'You're both as daft as each other,' Dorrie observed, stirring sugar into her tea. 'She does love that doll, though. Not bad from a pair of old stockings and scraps from the rag bag, eh, Tess?'

'So what delights have you conjured up for my daughter this year?' Bertie enquired. 'Should I have my toolbox at the ready?'

'Depends. Can you knock up a rabbit hutch?' Tessa smiled at the look of horror in her friend's eyes. 'No need to fret, I've not bought her a real rabbit.'

'Shame. That would have been tomorrow's dinner taken care of.'

Bertie's eyes twinkled, but he lowered his voice as they heard the patter of Anne's footsteps coming across the hall.

'Joke, Tess. I'd never eat a pet of our Anne's, but if this rationing don't let up soon, Mary's days might be numbered.'

With ears as sharp as a donkey's, Anne went straight to stand before her father's armchair, hands on her hips as she shook her head at him sternly, making her curls bob.

'What you said about Mary, Daddy?'

'I said poor old Mary must be worn out,' Bertie replied. 'Big day she's had today. Party and presents and being a whole year older.'

'That's me, silly,' Anne corrected him. 'And I'm not tired yet.'

Tessa smiled to herself as she watched little Anne get the better of her father. Times like this, when they were all together, she was always made to feel like a part of their family. Bertie she'd known since childhood, Dorrie, too, and Lil she'd hit it off with the moment they'd met on Lil's arrival in Birmingham six years ago. With Matthew missing, Tessa's family would remain incomplete, but she was fond of the Coopers, especially Anne, her goddaughter.

'Go and ask Auntie Tess where your present is,' Bertie encouraged his daughter.

'I not spoilt, Daddy. That's naughty to

ask for presents.' But a childlike curiosity glimmered in her eyes all the same as she turned towards the armchair where Tessa was sitting, the as yet unopened present hidden behind a cushion.

'You're quite right, Anne. Lucky it's not Daddy's birthday or he'd be getting no presents at all, would he?' She reached behind her to retrieve the cuddly rabbit she'd so painstakingly stitched from a brown velour hat. 'Tell you what. Close your eyes and hold your hands out.'

Obediently Anne squeezed her eyes shut and Tessa dropped to her knees on the carpet, shuffling closer to place the present into her upturned palms.

'He's a bunny rabbit!' Anne declared, having torn off the paper to reveal the soft animal with his polished button eyes and braided ribbon collar.

'Mary really wanted a bunny rabbit!' Cuddling him tight, she raised sparkling green eyes to Tessa. 'Thanks ever so, Auntie Tess.'

'You're welcome, poppet,' Tessa said softly. 'What will you call him?'

Anne considered this for a minute, then her face lit up. 'She's not a him, she's a her, and I going to call her Rosie. Rosie Rabbit.'

'Grand choice of name, my dear,' Bertie declared, getting to his feet and crossing to the mantel to turn on the wireless. 'A little music to mark the occasion, do we think? Bit of Flanagan & Allen, perhaps?'

'Bertram Cooper, you're not too old for my sharp tongue.' Dorrie chuckled as Anne whirled Rosie Rabbit around the room to the accompaniment of Glenn Miller.

Taking the small hand Anne held out to her, Tessa joined in with the impromptu dance; Bertie was already waltzing around the table and Dorrie took little persuasion to tap her feet and sway in time to the music.

'Bit of a lark without me, is it?' Lil's voice, cold and clipped, cut across the merriment like a knife through butter. 'Proper family you look as well. Perhaps I should have stayed in the bathroom and let you get on with it.'

Bertie snapped off the wireless, plunging the room into silence.

'Blimey, Lil, it's our Anne's birthday. Look, come and sit yourself down, have a cup of tea.' He turned to Anne. 'Go show Rosie to Mummy.'

Clutching the rabbit in her arms, Anne went silently to the chair into which Lil lowered her ample frame.

'She's called Rosie,' she said a little hesitantly. 'Auntie Tess made her for me.'

'Did she now?' A cursory glance over the rabbit and Lil's eyes were cold once more as she stared at Tessa. 'Talent coming out her ears, your auntie Tessa's got.'

'Takes no talent to sift through other people's cast-offs,' Tessa said. 'Talking of which, I'd better get cracking.'

In truth she had an hour yet before she had to leave, but if she was causing offence to Lil for some reason, she'd traipse the streets rather than risk upsetting Anne.

She wouldn't take it personally, she decided. Lil's mood dipped and soared like two planes in a dogfight, it couldn't be helped at the moment, with her being as fed up and uncomfortable as she was. For the life of her she seemed unable to find a smile; little wonder she'd resented the sight of them all so merry and laughing together.

But they were Lil's family. While Tessa wandered aimlessly through the park, a lonely figure filling in time before her shift at the town hall, Lil would be at the heart of her family. She'd be tucking Anne, and Rosie Rabbit, too, no doubt, into bed, she'd tiptoe out from her daughter's room to drink the waiting cup of tea Dorrie pressed into her hand, and after her mother-in-law had tactfully retired early to bed with a good book, she'd be cuddled up by the fire with Bertie, who adored his young wife so much that no matter how low her mood dropped, he'd never stop trying to make their world as she wished it.

Surrounded by such a close family, Tessa had never felt so alone.

* * *

They'd been right, the likes of Vince Watkins, and the pompous tones of the chaps who read the news bulletins, much of their usual stiffness dissolved in their excitement; once the Germans had lost their leader it had been a matter of days.

A week after Anne's birthday, on May 7, an announcement was broadcast at twenty to eight in the evening. They were all home, Lil and Bertie, Dorrie and Tessa, clustered around the wireless and hardly daring to breathe as the news they'd wished for was announced.

The war in Europe was over.

Lil and Bertie clung together, and Dorrie hugged them both. For Tessa all three of them spared a quick squeeze, but in her heart she felt cold.

Conflict in the Far East was continuing. Matthew was still flying bombing missions over there.

The war hadn't done with him yet.

A New Arrival

'I was starting to think that the rain would never let up!' Dorrie Cooper exclaimed, setting down the chair she'd been carrying to squint up at a grey sky brightening as shafts of sunlight began to break through. 'Here's hoping this fine weather holds.'

'Reckon it'll make no odds if the heavens open and we're all drowned rats in seconds,' Tessa commented, observing the bustle of activity as all along Hockley Street folk dragged out tables and chairs, hung decorations and draped bunting for one of the many street parties Birmmgham was to host that afternoon. 'If the war didn't beat us, a drop of rain's got no chance.'

Preparations had been in full swing since the night before. Moments after Churchill had confirmed the end of hostilities in Europe, and with it the announcement that the following two days were to be public holidays, across the city folk had wandered out into the streets, dazed, bewildered, delirious with joy and relief.

Having wandered out to sit on the front steps of the shop for a moment to herself, Tessa had watched the revelry for a while. Over garden walls tales of wartime heroics had been swapped and mugs of tea and glasses of ale, too, had been clinked together. Someone had wheeled out a gramophone and suddenly the still night air had crackled into life with popular records, to which a good many had danced and sung their hearts out. Someone else had hit upon the idea of shinnying up a lamppost to start hanging the red, blue and white bunting so faithfully purchased in anticipation of this moment, and he'd quickly been joined by others until the length of Hockley Street was draped in victory colours.

Heavy rain overnight had left the bunting decidedly bedraggled, but with the reappearance of a golden sun no-one seemed to mind all that much.

Spirits had risen once more, with all from young to old helping transform Hockley Street into one communal party.

End-to-end tables were being placed, laden with hastily made sandwiches and cakes fresh from the stoves of house-wives who'd thrown caution to the winds and pooled their entire rations of fat and sugar. Once more the air was filled with music as record after record was played on someone's gramophone.

There was no doubt about it, Tessa thought; a party was what the good folk of Birmingham wanted and a party was what they would have, come rain or shine.

'Wonder if Bertie's talked his way into borrowing that piano?' Dorrie wondered, to which Tessa smiled .

'Your Bertie could charm the birds out the trees, Dorrie. Poor old Jeannie's got no chance. He'll not be coming back without it.'

'I'm just thankful the Black Horse is but a street or two away,' Dorrie commented. 'Last thing we need is Bertie laid up with a bad back when Lil's past her due date.'

'Baby's been hanging on for the end of the war,' Tessa suggested, but she could only drum up the faintest of smiles as she stood for a moment and watched the growing excitement around her.

She was relieved it was over, of course she was. Her spirits had risen along with everyone else's. But she'd not be dancing in the streets, not yet.

'You heard from Matthew yet, Tess?' Dorrie asked as they headed back into the house. 'He'll be getting some time off, will he?'

Tessa swallowed.

'He telephoned this morning. They're having a forty-eight-hour stand-down.'

'There you go then, gel. He'll have plenty of time to pop back and see you.' Dorrie beamed at her. 'Even if it's just for a few hours, it's better than nothing. Tess? Isn't it?'

'It would be,' Tessa agreed, trying hard to keep her voice light, but to her own ears she could hear the tremble. 'He's not coming back. Some knees-up they're having on the base. Squadron solidarity, he's their lead officer.'

'He's your husband,' Dorrie countered bluntly, but seeing Tessa's distressed expression, her tone softened. 'I'm sorry, Tess, I'll not keep on about it. You know Matthew loves the bones of you. Reckon he's just been living and breathing the air force to the point it's messed up his loyalties. He'll be home soon enough and you'll have a whole life together.'

Tessa nodded.

'I know. It just would have been nice to see him.'

'You will, Tess. Before you know it.' Dorrie reached an arm around her shoulders. 'Shall we go and have a cup of tea? I could do with checking on that cake.'

She'd known straight away. As soon as the telephone trilled earlier that morning, she'd known it was Matthew. To hear his voice when she'd no idea from day to day if he was all right, it had seemed symbolic somehow, to hear that he was in one piece, today of all days. He'd survived the war this far, he'd not suffered as much as a scratch. He'd come through the rest of it unscathed, he would — he had to.

She'd sagged with relief, dropped down on to the chair in the hall and cradled the receiver against her ear. It had been a bad line, all crackly and broken up, but she'd heard clear as a bell the words that had made her heart break.

When she'd hung up, she'd sat there a good few moments more, trying to be sensible, to think logically about it. Really there was little point in Matthew leaving the base if it would only be for a few hours, and with him and his squadron remaining on alert for the next mission out East, it made sense that he stay where he could be called upon at a moment's notice.

'It will hurt, Tess,' he'd pointed out. 'If I come back now we'll have to say goodbye all over again in a matter of hours. Best we wait 'til it's for ever.'

He'd hesitated, waiting for a crackle in

the line to clear. 'I love you, Tess,' he'd said quietly. 'You know I do.'

She did know that, she knew exactly how much Matthew loved her, because she loved him the same. So much that if the boot were on the other foot, she'd have been on that train.

Tessa would have moved mountains if it meant she got to see Matthew. But she was here lugging chairs and making cakes while he was drinking and playing cards shoulder to shoulder with his RAF comrades, and later sharing a dance or three with the Air Transport women stationed nearby in High Wycombe.

Not that she worried for one moment he'd not be faithful to her. She knew she could trust Matthew. But he should be here with her. If he was to dance with anyone, it should be Tessa. Without him she wouldn't be dancing one tiny step. Even if the whole of Hockley Street broke into a conga, she'd take no part in it.

'Would you look at that?' Dorrie exclaimed, retrieving her sponge cake from the stove and placing it lovingly on to a plate to cool. 'Proper cake, made with sugar and butter, and not a sign of grated carrot anywhere. That's what you call a victory day treat.'

'You might,' Lil returned dryly, 'if you'd a hope of seeing a slice of it. Like gannets, that lot are. You take it out there and you'll not be swallowing so much as a crumb.'

'There's enough of us baking,' Dorrie assured her breezily. 'Cakes will be coming out our ears, don't you fret over that.'

'I wasn't,' Lil said. 'Thought of all that butter turns my stomach.' She shifted uncomfortably in her seat at the kitchen table. 'Where's Bertie gone off to?'

'The Black Horse,' Tessa cut in before Dorrie had chance. 'He's gone to badger Jeannie for a lend of the piano.'

'Planning on rolling it all the way back here, is he?' Lil enquired wryly. 'He'd better hope I don't start having the baby any time soon or he'll have to abandon his precious piano in the middle of

Brum.'

'You'll not have it that quick,' Dorrie told her. 'Babies give you a fair bit of warning. Our Anne took her time, if you remember.'

'I'm not about to forget, am I?' Lil snapped. 'Looks like this one's after copying its big sister and all. Is there any tea on the go, Tess?'

'Kettle's on,' Tessa said. 'You want a cup, Dorrie?'

'Day's not yet come when I'll say no to a cuppa.' With the baking tray scrubbed, Dorrie wiped her hands on a tea towel and sat down beside her daughter-in-law. 'I shall write a few lines to Bea while I've a moment. Fingers crossed she'll be stood down from the WAAF any day now. Be nice for you, won't it, Lil? An extra pair of hands with the new babby?'

'Smashing, yes,' Lil agreed. 'Auntie Bea's one in a million.'

Distracted by her search in the odds and ends drawer for a pen, Dorrie made no response, or perhaps she just judged it wise to keep her mouth shut, Tessa thought. Shame Lil couldn't do the same, but then Lil had the excuse of feeling more out of sorts with every day that passed with no baby. When she'd first met Bea Cooper, Bertie's twin sister, Lil had got on like a house on fire with her. Chances are she would again, once she was feeling halfway normal, but in the meantime Tessa knew the pedestal on which Dorrie placed her daughter was a sore point. You'd not see the likes of Beatrice Doreen Cooper, officer in the Women's Air Force and expert in radar signals and telegraphic operation, grumbling her way through pregnancy and then failing to have the baby on the right day.

Tessa had planned to enlist in the WAAF with Bea. She'd been friends with her since childhood. It had always been the four of them, Tessa and Matthew, Bertie and Bea, playing out in the street under Dorrie's watchful eye because old Esme Lane didn't give two hoots where they were as long as they were out from under her feet. And Matthew's older sister, Hilary, who'd become a substitute mother of sorts for him and Tessa, was far too busy running around after her cantankerous old mother to have much time to spare for anyone else.

They'd looked after each other, all four of them, but especially Tessa and Matthew. Years later, when he'd learned of her plans to join up, he'd been so distressed at the prospect that she'd let him talk her out of it.

Manning barrage balloons on an air base in Norfolk had been all well and good for Bea, but Matthew wanted Tessa to stay in the comparative safety of the home she knew.

Of course, back then none of them knew what the war had in store for Birmingham, how devastated the city would be by the nights of bombing towards the end of 1940.

She'd come through the lot unharmed, well, physically anyway.

Emotionally she'd taken a battering. Her mother-in-law she'd never been close to because an iceberg would thaw quicker than old Esme Lane, though it had knocked Tessa for six all the same when she'd been killed, but it was Hilary she went to pieces over, Hilary she still missed every day.

She'd been as good as a mother to Tessa, she'd still been a shoulder for her when they'd all grown up a bit and Hilary had her own daughter.

'You'll be sending for young Victoria now it's all over and done with, will you, Tess?' Her letter to Bea signed and sealed, Dorrie glanced up enquiringly at Tessa. 'With a bit of luck we can arrange it so Bea picks her up on route. Save you forking out for a train fare.'

'Thanks, but it should be me who goes to get her,' Tessa decided. 'I don't want Victoria fretting she's being a bother. I'll write a note to Peg in a bit, tell her I'm coming.'

'Gran'll miss having her around,' Lil said. 'She appreciates the company.'

Victoria had been a small child of just eight who'd not have said boo to a goose when, on Esme Lane's say-so, she'd been wrenched away from Hilary and packed off to the countryside, and what would remain her billet for the entirety of the war — a little cottage that was the home of Granny Peg, Lil's own grandmother.

Less than two years later she'd become an orphan overnight when Hilary was killed, her husband, Victoria's father, having already perished some months earlier on the beaches at Dunkirk. The only family Victoria had left in the world was her uncle Matthew and his wife.

Yet another Lane to squash in under the Coopers' roof.

Tessa glanced worriedly at Lil.

'Will that be all right, Lil? If Victoria moves in here?'

'Have to be, won't it?' Lil stated bluntly. 'She's got nowhere else to live. Need a medal, you do, Tess. Taking on someone else's kid without a word said about it.'

'She's Matthew's niece,' Tessa reasoned. 'I'm not about to turn my back on her. We're all she's got left.'

'Poor little mite, losing her mum and dad within months of each other.' Dorrie sighed. 'She's lucky she's got you to step in, Tess.'

Time would tell, Tessa thought. A poor little mite Victoria might have been back then, but she'd grown up a fair bit since. Fourteen she was now, a teenager good and proper, with all the fusses and grumbles and mood swings that went with it, and Victoria had more right than most to be difficult.

Granny Peg did a grand job as her substitute mother, but then Granny Peg had raised two daughters of her own, and a granddaughter. Each time Tessa had been to visit over the past few years, she'd seen first-hand how settled Victoria was living with the old lady, how naturally she looked to her for guidance and affection.

It had been a relief to know she was all right, happy even. If the opposite were true Tessa would have brought her home years ago, war or no war. But Victoria had come to love her life in the country. She had friends at the village school, she was doing well in her lessons, and at home she had two young cats she adored, borne of Mrs Whiskers, Granny

Peg's affable old tabby, and presented to Victoria as her very own.

She'd want to bring them back, of course she would, and Tessa wasn't about to argue — Victoria had seen enough loss in her life — but Hazel and Scrapes were used to having a big back garden to run around in. Where would they run around here in Hockley Street?

Same could be said of their owner, Tessa thought grimly. Victoria was used to wide, green, open spaces, to clear blue skies and feeling the sun on her head. Her room at Granny Peg's cottage, Lil's old room, took up most of the top floor; up in the eaves she had a window that looked out over miles of fields and trees and animals.

How would she adapt to sleeping in a room half the size, with a tiny window that looked out over demolished buildings, smoke damage, housing plots that were no more than littered wastelands, factory chimneys choking the sky with industrial smog? How would Victoria cope with the greyness of Birmingham?

'On your marks, get set, go!'

The flag Anne clutched in her fist was a blur of red, white and blue as Bertie helped her sweep it through the air, prompting the straggly line of excited children balancing apples on spoons to surge forwards.

'Daft as a brush, that son of mine,' Dorrie commented fondly, wiping her hands on her pinny as she straightened from handing out apples. 'Don't know who's more excited — him or them kids.'

'We've all got a dose of high spirits tonight, Dorrie,' Tessa reasoned, but her heart twisted a little as she watched Bertie hoist his daughter up on to his shoulders.

Lifted above a sea of heads, with a bird's eye view of the apple and spoon race, Anne waved her flag and cheered, excitement shining in her olive-green eyes.

She was just one of hundreds who crowded the length of Hockley Street, of every street in Birmingham, waving flags and cheering, crying with relief that it was all over. The night air sang with euphoria as gramophones crackled and eagerly built bonfires purged the city of its rubble.

Children raced and played, and couples danced and held each other close.

Pulling her cardigan tight around her, Tessa stood to one side, watching the merriment.

It was hard to believe that, a little over a week ago, the country had still been at war. For a good many in Hockley Street, the dark clouds seemed to have lifted. They'd not be waiting on anyone then, they couldn't be. Perhaps their husbands were released from duty, were home and safe.

Perhaps it was just Matthew still off fighting a war.

'Come and have a drink, Tess.' Dorrie rested a hand briefly on her arm. 'Wireless is going on in a bit, ready for when King George makes his speech.'

Unless he was going to announce there'd been a change of plan, and no more bombs were to be dropped over the

Far East, meaning Matthew could come home, Tessa couldn't think why she'd want to listen to a word of it, but she just nodded, and followed Dorrie across the road to the pavement outside Li'l Tessa's, where Lil was sitting on a chair, looking as awkward and uncomfortable as if she'd been perched on a wooden ledge and left there to stew.

'Our Anne's not seen a night as late as this since she was a baby,' she remarked as Tessa dragged a chair closer to hers and sank on to it. 'She'll be half asleep come tomorrow morning, and he —' She nodded her head towards Bertie, who was bouncing Anne up and down on his shoulders, '—he can see to her, because it's not me who's got her so wound up she'll not sleep a wink, is it?'

'If she was in bed she'd not be sleeping,' Tessa reasoned. 'Not with all this music and mayhem going on.'

Lil glanced at her.

'I'm not the only one who thinks this is a right palaver, then. Mind you, something tells me you'd be dancing and clapping with the rest of them if Matthew had carted himself back here for five minutes. What's that squadron got that you don't, for goodness' sake?'

'Matthew,' Tessa said simply.

'He's barmy, if you ask me,' Lil continued. 'Chance to turn his back on the war for a few hours and he stays cooped up with it. He's not the only daft one round here, mind.' Once more her gaze settled on to Bertie, who was carefully perching their daughter on top of the piano he'd rolled all the way from the Black Horse. 'Hope someone's had word in the King's ear. He can't go making speeches bang in the middle of Bertie's sing-song.'

Tessa smiled faintly.

'The very thought.'

With minutes to go before King George's message was due to be broadcast, Bertie struck up the opening chords of a popular ditty, his daughter singing and clapping her hands in time with the music.

It would have made Bertie's night, Tessa thought; Lil's, too, though she'd not have admitted it in a month of Sundays; if all three were to sing together, if Lil would just dredge up the energy to haul herself out of her chair, even if once she reached the piano she sat back down again. Just for her to be at Bertie's side like she used to, singing her heart out, it would have meant more to him than the end of the war itself.

'Anne takes after you, Lil,' Tessa said. 'Voice of an angel, she's definitely her mother's daughter.'

But Lil's expression was resolute as she turned her attention to the cup of tea Dorrie placed into her hand.

'I hope not,' she said so quietly it was almost a whisper, a wish she didn't dare utter out loud in case to do so would shatter it. 'Not all that for her, Tess. Not for my Anne.'

When Tessa thought about it afterwards, much later that night, when it was quieter as even the most ardent of revellers were packing up their gramophones, she couldn't quite piece together how it had happened, what had set Lil off. One minute she'd barely whispered her darkest fear, the next she'd upended a whole cup of tea, scalding both her own hands and Tessa's.

Had it been the shock of it? Or maybe it had just been time, and it was the pain, sudden and violent, that sent her tea flying and brought Bertie running, piano abandoned in the middle of Hockley Street.

Tessa had barely noticed the way her hands smarted. With Anne clinging to her, she'd given no thought to anything else. It was up to her to calm the little girl's fears, to reassure her that Mummy wasn't poorly, she just had a bit of a stomach ache because it was hard work bringing a new baby brother or sister into the world.

'I want a baby brother,' Anne had decided. 'I want to dress him up and wheel him around in Mary's pram.'

They'd missed the King's speech in the end. Nine o'clock his message had been broadcast to the nation, and it was not Bertie's musical repertoire but his new son's lungs that had given King George a run for his money.

Anne had got her wish; at one minute past nine her new baby brother had taken his first breath.

'Born on Victory Day,' Bertie had murmured, bewildered, as he watched his son snuggle into Lil's arms. 'There's only one name he can have.'

Limp with exhaustion, Lil had managed a thin smile as briefly her eyes met Bertie's.

'Victor,' she'd whispered. 'Victor Bertram Cooper.'

The front steps outside Li'l Tessa's weren't all that comfortable, not without a cushion anyway. Back when they'd first bought the business, and spent every spare minute doing it up, repainting walls; knocking up shelves and arguing over which Tessa Lane originals the mannequins in the window would model, Tessa and Lil had brought a cup of tea and a biscuit and sat out on the steps, taken just five minutes' break to watch the world go by.

In the small hours of the morning, when the absolute darkness was starting to recede, Tessa sat alone on the steps, watching her breath fog out in front of her.

She couldn't sleep. For the life of her she couldn't drift off. Not down to Victor's crying, not now anyway. He'd worn himself out and was sleeping soundly. As were his parents, and even his proud big sister, over-excited as she was, had finally given in and closed her eyes.

For a few precious hours until Victor awoke and demanded his breakfast, number 27, Hockley Street was still and peaceful.

In the street outside, yards of patriotic bunting flapped in the dawn breeze, and the odd flag, dropped by a child, perhaps, billowed a little way across the road, coming to land in a puddle of ale, where it fluttered pathetically for a moment before lying still.

Charred embers of hastily erected bonfires soured the air, the scent of cremated belongings, of the debris of a war. Tessa's hands were smarting. Soon as she'd had a chance she'd run a bowl of cold water and soaked them, but she'd left it too long and her skin was red and sore.

Bringing her palms to rest gingerly upon the cold stone of the step, she gritted her teeth against the initial shock of it. She was being silly, getting upset over a bit of a sting. Lil had suffered far worse pain tonight. But her eyes filled with tears as she sat and gazed up at a cloudless sky, watching the stars.

'See that one there? That's 'Ye Old Grand Wishing Star',' Matthew had told her solemnly, on the night of their wedding, when they'd sat side by side on the back doorstep, just like they'd always done. 'Wish on it and whatever you wish will always come true.'

Tessa had grinned at him.

'You don't half come up with some rubbish, Matthew.'

'Long as it makes you smile I'd best keep doing it, hadn't I?' He'd taken her hand in his and squeezed it affectionately. Then he'd looked at her the way that made her feel he was seeing deep into her, right through to the bone. 'Wish on it anyway, Tess. Miles apart we might be, but when we look up there we'll be seeing the same sky.'

They'd sat there a good while after that, quietly content to be in each other's company, just watching the stars and holding hands.

Six years later, every wish she'd made had been granted. He'd stayed safe and unharmed — he'd made it through the war this far. There was just one more she needed to make, to bring him home to her.

With no hand to hold but her own, Tessa entwined one with the other.

'Matthew,' she whispered. 'I wish for you.'

Now What?

Tessa rested her forehead against the train window, heedless of the grimy glass as she watched the fresh, green hues of the Welsh countryside rattle past.

It seemed to her they'd not long left the smoke and bustle of New Street but already it felt like another world outside, a world obscured by the heavy cloud of war. With the city behind her, she looked upon banks of yellow primroses, apple-blossom, elms and copper beech trees, and bluebell woods that glinted indigo in the morning sunshine.

It was oddly reassuring, Tessa mused. While the likes of Birmingham were littered with carcasses of homes and buildings reduced to smouldering bricks and rubble, miles and miles of countryside were unspoilt by the bombings. A reminder that in places the world was as it once was, and how it would be once more.

To all sides of her the carriage was

alight with the animated, and sometimes raucous, voices of servicemen and
women stood down from duty and making the journey back to their loved ones.
The train was packed tight; not a seat in
this carriage nor any other was free, and
the spaces between were filled with folk
so relieved to be going home they'd have
strapped themselves to the roof if they'd
had to.

Clutching her handbag on her lap,
Tessa returned her attention to the passing fields, the hills that rose higher the
further into Wales they travelled, the
cows and the sheep that grazed content-
edly.

She'd made this journey many times.
So often had her destination been
Hawarden, and the RAF base where
Matthew had spent all those months,
that even though he'd been transferred
from there a year since, her heart still
gave a little leap as she recognised familiar landmarks.

Her destination today was not all that
far beyond Hawarden, and one to which

she'd travelled as many times.

Today she was on her way to fetch Victoria.

There was no reason to dally; now that peace had been declared and it was officially safe for Victoria to walk the streets of Birmingham once more, she had no further need to remain in her countryside billet. She was Matthew's niece and her place was home in Hockley Street with Tessa.

'Sit yourself down, gel,' Peg urged an hour later when Tessa arrived at the back door of her cottage. 'I'll have that kettle brewing in two shakes. Train packed, were it?'

'Like sardines,' Tessa confirmed, unwinding the scarf from around her shoulders. 'Forgive me turning up out of the blue like this, Peg. I should have written first.'

Peg harrumphed scornfully as she set a full kettle on to the hob and lit the gas beneath.

'Post being what it is round these parts, you're as well to just catch a train and be done with it. You'll be staying tonight, will you?'

'I've money in my purse for a room at the village inn,' Tessa assured her, knowing even as she spoke the words that Peg wouldn't hear of it, that she'd insist as she always did that it would be no trouble to make up the spare bed.

Peg nodded, her eyes firmly on the tea caddy as she ladled spoonfuls into the pot with precision.

'For the best this time, if you'll not take offence, Tess.'

'Of course not,' Tessa managed, but she was taken aback at such an unexpected response.

For six years she'd visited Victoria as frequently as she'd been able, and each and every time she'd arrived to a warm welcome from Peg, and instant scorn poured on the notion that she would sleep anywhere but under the old lady's roof. Tessa was family, Peg always pointed out, she was Victoria's family and as such she should be permitted to spend as much time as was possible with her and not be relegated to some poky room in a cheap and draughty inn.

'I'm all at sixes and sevens, you see,' Peg explained, as she ferreted around in the cupboard for the biscuit barrel. 'What with Victoria's friends kipping in the spare room, an' them cats of hers have got the run of the place an' all, pair of 'em sit over that hearth like queens on a throne. Here we are, I knew I'd a few ginger biscuits lurking about.'

'I hope you know how grateful Matthew and I are to you, Peg,' Tessa ventured. 'You've taken Victoria in and looked after her as if she were one of your own.'

Peg beamed with pride.

'That's how I think of her, Tess. She's a treasure. No trouble at all. As much a part of this cottage as this here table, is our Victoria.'

'I expect you'll miss her,' Tessa said quietly. 'Be nice to have your home to yourself again, though, children and cats out from under your feet.'

'Six years since it were that quiet,' Peg

mused, taking up a cloth to lift the whistling kettle off the hob. 'Will you fetch the milk from the pantry, Tess?'

Wandering through to the tiny pantry, Tessa's mind was troubled as she sought out the milk can.

As yet she'd not put into words her intention to take Victoria home with her tomorrow, but surely Peg realised that would happen? The war was over — Victoria had no further need of a safe billet. She was Matthew's niece, and by marriage Tessa's, too. They were the family with whom she belonged.

But after six years of Victoria's company, Peg would be bound to miss her. It was little wonder she seemed so reluctant to talk of her departure.

Maybe it was for the best that Tessa would be staying at the inn tonight, the last night that Victoria was to live under Granny Peg's roof. She would perhaps appreciate the chance to share a last few hours with the old lady who, these past few years, had been the closest thing to a mother she'd known.

She'd not deny either of them that, Tessa decided, as she lifted the milk can and strode purposefully back into the kitchen. After all, by tomorrow night Victoria would be back in Birmingham, where she belonged.

Even if Peg's reluctance to make up the spare bed this time really was a need to have Victoria to herself for one more evening, after the devoted care she'd given her, it was a small price to pay.

'Victoria should be home soon,' Peg announced, lifting the cosy and mashing the tea. 'She's late more evenings than not, mind.'

'Why's that?' Tessa glanced at the clock on the dresser. 'She's not in bother at school, is she?'

'Gracious, no.' Peg chuckled. 'She'll be helping the younger children with them vegetable patches they've got up and running. Country lass good and proper, she is now. Happy as Larry up to her ears in soil and spuds. She's milk monitor, too, you know,' she added proudly, as if she were extolling the virtues of her own child. 'Them littl'uns think the world of her.'

'She'll be a natural with our Anne then,' Tessa concluded. 'Reckon she'll take a shine to Victor, too. Happy chap, he is. Strong pair of lungs on him, mind. When he wants feeding the whole of Brum knows about it.'

'Lil were the same when she were a babby,' Peg reflected. 'Her ma always said she were practising for the stage. Starting early so she'd be hitting them top notes before she were out of nappies.' She sipped her tea thoughtfully, eyeing Tessa over the rim of her cup. 'She still singing down that pub?'

'The Black Horse,' Tessa supplied. 'Been a while, but she's got Anne, and now the new babby to think of.'

'Her ma were playing to packed out pubs while Lil were asleep in her crib in the back room,' Peg countered stubbornly. 'Singing's in her blood, Tess. She needs it, same as her ma did, and her auntie, too.' She smiled, a wistful expression softening her features. 'Wales's answer to the Andrews Sisters, clustered round my old piano night after night, an' Lil's face lit up like a Christmas tree, the way it still does every time she sings her heart out.'

Tessa knew as well as Peg how it lifted Lil's spirits the second she sung the first note, but she would speak not one word against her friend as if the decision to cast aside her music had been made on a whim.

'She's a good mum, Lil is,' she remarked.

'Not for one minute did I think she weren't. She's had a heart o' gold since she were a littl'un. Downside to that, though, Tess, she feels everything ten times more than's necessary.' She fixed sharp eyes on Tessa. 'That'll be why she's knocked the singing on the head, will it? Got herself all caught up in a lather over this mothering lark, an' heaven knows why when she's you an' Bertie, an' that ma of his, who by all accounts trips over herself to help.

'There's folk in worse predicaments

than Lil — this war's seen to that.'

'I think it's all a bit overwhelming,' Tessa suggested, choosing her words carefully. 'Her new life with Bertie, then the shop, and now she's two children dependent on her for everything.'

'What she wanted,' Peg declared bluntly. 'Never seen her as happy as when she tied the knot with her Bertie. Babbies aren't babbies for ever, it's not worth getting in a dither about.' She pushed the biscuit barrel towards Tessa. 'Have another, Tess. You look as though you're wasting away. So how's business at the shop anyway? Thought this were supposed to be your big venture, the pair of you? Is it not paying back what you put in?'

Tessa swallowed a lump of ginger biscuit that felt like dust in her mouth.

'What Lil put in,' she corrected her. 'Her Aunty Mai's legacy funded Li'l Tessa's, Peg.'

'And there'd be nowt to fund if it were left to Lil to stock the shelves,' Peg pointed out. 'You're the talent, Tess. My

Lil can hold her own with a sewing-machine these days but it's you who dreams up the next creation.'

'Then it's down to me that we've only a trickle of customers.' Tessa sighed. 'Nothing in the window to tempt them through the door, and more of Lil's money going on rent when I'm years away from paying her back.'

She was surprising herself with how easy she found it to talk to Peg about this. To Lil's own grandmother she was admitting how hard she feared it would be for Lil to recoup her investment in the shop, the money that had only been hers in the first place because she'd been left it in her Auntie's will. Marianne, who'd been Peg's eldest daughter.

Tessa's dressmaking talent she'd inherited from her own mother, but that she had a premises in which to showcase it had been down to Lil, and the faith she'd shown in committing her Aunty Mai's money.

Tessa felt as though she was in debt to the whole family.

Maybe that was why she so willingly confided in Peg. She needed someone to assure her she was not merely a drain on their finances but a continued safe bet, and who would tell her straight better than the forthright, plain-spoken matriarch of the family?

'Times as they are, folk haven't had two pennies to rub together,' Peg reminded her. 'But now their menfolk are coming home women'll be wanting something pretty. You might find your fortunes change for the better, Tess.'

'I've been counting on that,' Tessa agreed.

'It's after that you've to think on,' Peg cautioned her. 'When the euphoria dies down an' folk start the long haul of getting back to their lives. If it's anything like the last war, be a while yet before the economy picks itself up. That'll be the test. If your shop can hold its own when the country's at its knees then you're on to a winner. If not, then that's the time to stop an' do your sums, Tess.'

She'd wanted a straight answer, Tessa

thought. There was none better suited than Peg for telling it how it was.

'You've a solid position at that factory?' Peg queried, and when Tessa nodded, 'Could be worse then, gel. Least you've an income separate from the shop.'

'Not enough to rent a house, though,' Tessa said flatly. 'If the shop fails I can't expect Lil to put me up for ever.'

'She'll not see you out on the streets,' Peg assured her. 'But I expect you'll be wanting your own space nonetheless, once your Matthew's stood down from the air force? Your own house just for the two of you.'

'Victoria, too,' Tessa added. 'She'll be living with us.'

'Of course,' Peg replied breezily, reaching across the table to lift the tea cosy once more. 'Top up, Tess?'

Moments later the back door finally opened and Victoria herself appeared, flinging her satchel on to a chair on her way to the sink to wash her hands. Focused on what she was doing, she'd not even glanced at Tessa. It couldn't have escaped her notice that Peg had company, Tessa thought, but she'd likely have dismissed it as just one of her friends from the village.

It seemed Peg was in no hurry to enlighten her, either.

'Good day at school, pet?'

Victoria shrugged.

'Same as every day, Gran. Got myself caked with mud helping them littl'uns with their digging.' She reached for a dry cloth and wiped her hands before finally turning to face them. 'That's got the worst of it, though. What's for tea, Gran? Oh, hello, Tess. What are you doing here?'

'Fine way to talk to your auntie, that is.' Tessa smiled as she stood up and took a step towards her niece, but the embrace she pulled Victoria into felt stiff and awkward. 'Hello, Victoria. How are you?'

'You know.' Another shrug, this time directed at Tessa, before Victoria turned once more to Granny Peg. 'How long before tea's ready? Have I got an hour to pop over to Jenny's and work on our history project? Miss Spencer wants it done by Friday.'

Peg glanced at the clock.

'I'd say you've an hour and not a minute more, my girl. So change out of that uniform and get cracking.'

'Thanks, Gran.' Victoria grinned, planting a kiss on the old lady's cheek as she dashed past to change her clothes.

An uneasy feeling was beginning to settle in the pit of Tessa's stomach. Peg must know why she was here, and yet she was talking to Victoria as though her young charge was going nowhere. Why permit her to work on a school project that was wanted in by Friday? She'd be home in Birmingham by Friday!

'Peg, I want Victoria to come home with me,' Tessa stated firmly. 'You must know how grateful we all are to you, but the war's over now. You've no need to look after her any more. When I leave tomorrow, I'm taking her with me.'

Peg looked at her gravely, and for a long moment.

'Of course you wish her to be home with you,' she said quietly. 'As you say, the war is over now and she should be home with her family. What's left of it anyway.'

'Matthew's her uncle, and by marriage I'm her auntie,' Tessa reasoned, but the feeling of unease was growing. 'We're her only living relatives.'

'Then of course it's down to you to take her in,' Peg concluded. 'Is Matthew still in active combat?'

'He's still flying out, yes,' Tessa replied quietly. 'But he'll be home soon.'

'This war's scattered folk to the winds!' Peg exclaimed. 'An' it's no sense of timing. There's Matthew still being sent up night after night an' here's our Victoria in the middle of her school year an' projects due left, right an' centre.'

'I've another one to do by the end of next week.' Catching the tail end of Peg's words as she sauntered back into the room, Victoria spoke cheerfully as she crammed a history book into her satchel. 'Miss Spencer's on about setting

72

us a practical task for science, and me and Jenny convinced her to let us write up the school gardens, and this whole digging for victory palaver.'

'You've worked hard on it, I'll say that for you,' Peg agreed, her eyes once more averted from Tessa's as she further delayed the moment when she would have to burst Victoria's bubble.

'Victoria,' Tessa said, firmly enough that her niece stopped in her tracks, one hand on the back doorknob as she swivelled round impatiently.

'I'll be late for Jenny's, Tess.'

'Two more minutes won't make much difference.'

She'd not mention how hurt she was that Victoria preferred the company of her friend to that of the aunt she'd not seen in months, Tessa decided. There was little point causing an upset over that. But Victoria must be told of Tessa's plans. If only because she'd want to say a last goodbye to Jenny before she left tomorrow.

'Can't we talk when I get back?' Victoria protested, but Tessa shook her head firmly.

'Victoria, I'm not just here for a fleeting visit. You know the war's over now. I've come to take you home.'

Tessa knew well enough how settled Victoria was here with Peg; indeed she'd been grateful for it; and she'd expected her to feel a little sad at having to leave the home she'd grown to love.

She didn't expect the defiance that flashed in Victoria's eyes, nor the plain hostility in her tone.

'I don't want to go back to Birmingham, Tess. I live here now.'

Tessa swallowed the panic rising in her chest.

'You were evacuated here, Victoria, to keep you safe. It was only ever a temporary arrangement.'

'I've lived here almost half my life,' Victoria stated. 'And Granny Peg likes having me here.'

'Be that as it may, your place is with your uncle Matthew and I,' Tessa persisted, having difficulty now in keeping the anger from her voice. 'We're your family. Besides, you can't impose on Granny Peg's hospitality indefinitely. The war's over, Victoria.'

'Is Uncle Matthew home then?' Victoria demanded. 'Why's he not here to fetch me? He's my proper family, you'd have no right to boss me around if you'd not married him.'

'Now then, Victoria,' Peg admonished her. 'There's nowt to be gained by talking to your auntie like that.'

But for once Victoria seemed unwilling even to heed her beloved Granny Peg.

'I have to finish this year at school,' she pointed out, her face lighting up with the knowledge she'd dragged up a failsafe argument. 'Can't just leave halfway through.'

'You're a little further than halfway through,' Tessa countered as patiently as she could. 'Anyway, there are schools in Birmingham, Victoria. It'll be no trouble to enrol you in one of them.'

'My friends are here,' Victoria said in a cold voice. 'And what about my cats?

Hazel and Scrapes will hate living in the city, they'll have nowhere to run. And Granny Peg, she'll miss me.'

'Granny Peg isn't your guardian,' Tessa said firmly.

'Neither are you.' Wilful, defiant, Victoria faced her with a rigid, resolute stare. 'If Uncle Matthew's not home yet, I don't have to be, either. I've got school, and it's important.' She hesitated, her tone dropping to a little above a whisper as she delivered what she clearly thought to be the definitive, closing argument. 'Mum wouldn't have made me leave.'

Later Tessa was to regret the words she spoke in that moment, the rebuke that escaped her in such a heated exchange, but the thought of returning to Birmingham without Victoria in tow, of knowing she'd failed to keep Matthew's family together, made her cruel as she glared at her niece.

'Your mum isn't here, though, is she?'

'I know that!' Victoria's eyes filled with tears as she slammed her beret down ferociously on her head. 'I'm going to Jenny's now, Gran. I'll stop for tea there — Jenny's mum won't mind.'

With that she turned on her heel and the door slammed behind her.

She felt Peg's arm slide around her shoulders.

'If it makes her happy to finish this year at school, I've no objection to keeping her a while longer,' she assured Tessa. 'She's been not a spot of bother to me.'

Tessa could hear the tremble in her voice as she glanced up at the old lady's face.

'She'll not have spoken to you in that way. But I dare say you'd not be so cruel as to bring up her mum as I did.'

'Anger makes us say things we regret.' Peg sighed. 'Victoria's in no doubt as to your affection for her, Tess. Given time, she'll want to be back with her family. Reckon it was a bit of a shock, you turning up like this.'

'I should have written first,' Tessa concluded flatly, and Peg patted her shoulder kindly.

'Aye, lass, perhaps you should. No

harm done, mind. What is it now? May? She's two months left of this school year, give or take a week or three. Is there a chance Matthew will be home before then? How about you take that time to prepare for both of them? Concentrate on pulling in business at the shop so you've a solid life for them to come back to. In the meantime Victoria can stay here with me and finish her studies,' she concluded, the satisfaction evident in her tone that she'd presented Tessa with a watertight compromise.

In much the same way as Victoria had sounded when she'd pointed out the obligation she had to remain here for the sake of her schooling. No wonder they were so close, Tessa thought wryly.

What choice did she have but to agree to Peg's suggestion? It was clear as a bell she'd not be dragging Victoria on to that train tomorrow with any ease, and to put her foot down was to land herself with a sullen, resentful child she'd not the slightest faith she could deal with.

'You'll stay for tea, won't you?' Peg

faltered, and Tessa thought she detected a trace of guilt in her voice, but by now she was too tired and defeated to care. 'Maybe I can make that spare room presentable.'

'Don't trouble yourself.' Wearily, Tessa got to her feet. 'Thank you, Peg, but I see no benefit in staying any longer. Victoria will calm a lot quicker if she finds only you here on her return.'

'You'll have something to eat at the inn then?'

Tessa smiled thinly as she wrapped her scarf once more around her throat.

'I shan't be stopping at the inn, Peg. There's a late train back to Birmingham. If I leave now I'll catch it.'

Peg opened her mouth as if to protest, but thought better of it. Instead she just nodded as she patted Tessa's arm.

'For the best, I think. Once Matthew's home, and Victoria's finished this year at school, it'll be a better time to fetch her. Until then she's a home here, you've no cause to fret on that.'

The train was late. Tessa pulled her

mother's coat tight around her shoulders, buttoning it up to the neck as she peered in vain into the distance, the absence of so much as a faint trace of smoke telling her plainly there was no train in sight.

There was one single wooden bench on the tiny country platform. She sank down on to it to wait. What else could she do? True, if the train failed to arrive, she could retrace her steps and book herself into the inn, but with no Victoria by her side she wanted only to get back to Birmingham.

She knew Matthew trusted her to watch over Victoria in his absence, to make the right decisions for her, to see that she was safe and well and happy.

She'd let him down. He trusted her and she'd let him down. She'd allowed her anger to get the better of her and she'd upset Victoria so much it was little wonder she was returning alone.

Matthew would come home to her now, and there'd be no Victoria there, and she'd have to tell him why, that she'd tried to fetch her home and failed.

She'd write to him, this evening, the moment she got home. Even if it was the wrong side of midnight and dark as coal, she'd light a candle and pour her heart out until her hand ached and her eyes were sore.

When he'd first left her to join the RAF, she'd tried to edit her letters to him so that they were bright and cheerful, so determined had she been to protect him from knowing anything less when he'd enough on his own plate without having her troubles to contend with, but Matthew had seen through her words straight away. He'd implored her to write to him as she'd always been able to talk to him. Every last word, no matter how grim or painful.

Matthew wanted to know Tessa as he always had, no matter how many miles separated them. And Tessa wanted to tell him. There was no-one she wanted to confide in more.

Some two hours past its scheduled arrival time, the train finally steamed into New Street station. Tired and emotional, and weak with hunger now, though she barely noticed it, Tessa allowed herself to be jostled amidst the throng of other passengers off the train and through the station, out into the street.

Some leapt quickly into waiting taxi cabs, others whistled and waved, doing their best to hail a passing cab. Though her bones ached, Tessa preferred to walk home. She'd no words for civil conversation with a cab driver; with the way the shop was faltering she had no spare pence for the fare, either.

It was a fair walk back to Hockley Street, but she knew Birmingham like the back of her hand, and what might have been a journey twice as long she shortened considerably by cutting through ginnels and across wastelands, the surefootedness of a cat ensuring she stepped free of scattered rubble and splintered glass.

In similar safety would Victoria walk home from Jenny's house, her own path blighted only by grass and flowers, and at worst the occasional pebble.

Was it any wonder she'd not wanted to return to this?

Outside number 27, Tessa hesitated a moment before she opened her bag to retrieve her key; Lamplight flickered in the windows upstairs, which meant Bertie at least, and possibly Lil, too, were still awake.

They'd be expecting her to return tomorrow, with Victoria in tow. The moment they heard her key in the lock, they'd want to know what had happened.

As yet she'd no energy to explain.

She'd sit on the steps a while, she decided. Perhaps they'd go to bed soon and she could tiptoe in and have the benefit of a night's sleep before she had to explain her unexpected presence in the morning.

If only she'd paper and pen with her, she could have started her letter to Matthew, written to him by moonlight. He'd have liked that.

A sudden movement in the corner of her eye made Tessa glance up sharply.

Someone was there.

Hockley Street, this late at night, was deserted. But someone was definitely there.

In her pocket Tessa's fingers curled determinedly around her torch, while her other hand searched frantically in her handbag for her keys.

'Hello?' A soft voice enquired, the owner of it at last emerging from the shadows. 'Are you Mrs Lane? Tessa?'

She was a young woman, perhaps a little younger than Tessa, and thin, worryingly so. In her arms, resting against her shoulder, she carried a bundle — a child, Tessa noted, as her eyes grew accustomed to the dark. A sleeping child, nestled against this young woman's shoulder maybe, but out at this hour, in the dark and the cold?

And how did she know who Tessa was? What did she want with her?

'I'm Tessa Lane, yes,' she confirmed. 'Might I ask who you are?'

The young woman stepped forward, into the dim light cast by the street lamp.

'I'd not meant to startle you,' she

began, the telltale soft Welsh lilt in her voice making it clear she didn't hail from Birmingham. 'My name is Iris Phelps.'

Tessa waited. Should the name mean something to her? Iris spoke as though it should, and yet for the life of her she could recall no-one by that name.

'Forgive me,' Tessa said as kindly as she could manage when all she really wished to do at this hour was retreat to her bed. 'You talk as though I should know you, and I'm afraid I don't.'

Iris looked confused, though she recovered her composure quickly.

'My mistake, Mrs Lane. Please accept my apologies. I've no business being here.'

Turning on her heel, she began to walk away, a solitary figure swiftly swallowed up by the darkness.

Tessa could have let her go. This Iris Phelps, whoever she might be, was of no concern to her. She was a stranger. Tessa had enough on her mind with her own family.

Yet she leapt to her feet, and she followed Iris Phelps into the shadows.

'Mrs Phelps? Iris? Can I be of any help to you? It's late and it's cold, and you have a child in your arms.'

Iris Phelps stopped suddenly, turning to face Tessa so there was now only inches of space between them. Tessa noted with growing alarm the dullness in her eyes, the dark shadows beneath them, and the lines that creased her brow.

'I'm not after charity,' she whispered, heeding the child in her arms who stirred in his sleep before nestling back against her shoulder. 'It's just . . . well, your husband . . . Matthew. He said he'd tell you about me.'

A Turn in Fortunes

'You know Matthew? My Matthew?' Bewildered, Tessa stared at Iris Phelps. Whoever she was, Matthew could have crossed paths with her easily enough — these past six years he'd been posted all over the place.

But he wrote to Tessa every week, more frequently if he could, and not one mention had he made of an Iris Phelps.

She'd believed they had no secrets from each other. Yet Iris was proof he'd kept at least one. So what else had he not told her?

They'd been separated for six long years. Had he found it harder and harder to be alone? Had he been so desperately lonely without Tessa that he'd fallen out of love with her and found another to take her place? Was that why he'd failed to mention Iris?

Was he having trouble finding the words that would break Tessa's heart?

No. Angry at herself, she shook her head, as if to dislodge such ridiculous thoughts. She was tired and emotional after having to leave Victoria. In her right mind she would know without question that Matthew was incapable of betraying her.

But for a long moment Iris Phelps offered no alternative explanation.

Instead she looked near enough ready to scarper, a wild and worried look in her eyes, but something compelled her to stand her ground.

Desperation, Tessa thought. Whatever her circumstances, one thing about Iris Phelps was clear. She'd fallen on to hard times, even harder than most. By the looks of her she was one of the many who'd lost all but the clothes on their backs. The city was crawling with them. Ex-service folk who'd returned from fighting to discover their homes burned to the ground, their jobs given to others and their lives unrecognisable.

Why else would she be out at this hour, with a child asleep in her arms?

'Would you like a cup of tea?' Tessa offered. 'We've a kitchen adjoining the shop. You can get yourself warm and, when you're ready, tell me what it is you came to say.'

Iris hesitated only a second before nodding.

'You're kind, Mrs Lane. Matthew said you would be.'

'He told you to come looking for me?'

'He said you'd help. He promised.'

Iris Phelps held her child tightly in her arms, waiting patiently while Tessa unlocked the door to the shop. Upstairs the lamp was still on, she'd noticed. She'd just have to run up quick and give them an edited version of events. It wouldn't do to leave Iris down here alone for longer than was absolutely necessary.

Not that Tessa was worried about the shop. For one thing Iris looked far too pale and exhausted to carry so much as a scarf further than the bottom of the steps, and besides, Matthew wouldn't send someone here who was remotely capable of robbing them blind.

Iris obviously needed help, and she'd worked up the courage to emerge from the shadows and ask for it. Tessa's conscience forbade her to linger more than a moment in Lil and Bertie's living-room.

'So this woman — this stranger — is lurking around our shop?' Lil exclaimed. 'You're barmy, Tess. On your shoulders be it if she empties the till and scarpers.'

'Give over, Lil,' Bertie chided her. 'Tessa's not daft.'

'Heavens, no,' Lil muttered. 'Perish the thought.'

'Might be a blessing in disguise, this,' Bertie suggested. 'Help Iris Phelps and it might just stop you dwelling on Victoria for five minutes, Tess.'

There was an element of truth in that, Tessa thought. Right now she'd give anything to not feel as small and useless as she did, to not have that niggling feeling, no matter how she tried to squash it, that she'd wronged Matthew because his niece was still living with a stranger.

She could make it up to him a little by helping Iris Phelps. If he'd directed her to Hockley Street he must know something of her predicament and he'd be trusting Tessa to help. This time she'd not let him down.

Leaving Lil and Bertie to their cups of tea in front of the fire, she hurried back down the stairs. She'd left Iris sitting on a chair in the kitchen, with the kettle boiling on the hob. She'd make them both a nice cup of tea and with any luck Iris would be relaxed enough to tell her story.

The kitchen was empty. On the hob the kettle was beginning to whistle but the chair Iris had occupied was tucked neatly back under the table.

Tessa turned off the gas and slipped quietly through to the shop.

Perhaps Iris had grown tired of waiting for her and was having a bit of a browse. But she knew already she'd not find her there.

Iris Phelps was gone.

★ ★ ★

'Not in my nature to say I told you so,' Lil began. 'So I won't. Don't need to, do

I? She'll be away with half the shop by now. We'll have to do an inventory in the morning, tot up what she's had.'

'She's had nothing,' Tessa answered her sharply. 'Have a look if you don't believe me. Anyway, where's she supposed to have stowed it? In her baby's blanket?'

Hands on her hips, Lil stood in the middle of the shop like a detective, her eyes visibly scrutinizing every shelf.

'That's another thing, Tess. What woman in her right mind has a babby out at this time of night?'

'A desperate one,' Tessa muttered. 'She might have nowhere else to go.'

'Not what she's taken we should be looking for then,' Lil remarked cryptically. 'But what she might have left behind. Her baby,' she added, when Tessa looked at her enquiringly. 'If she's any sort of mother she'll not want her child living on the street. She probably saw a chance to get him a better life; that was probably her plan all along.'

Tessa shook her head.

'You didn't see her, Lil. She was clinging to that baby like he was all she had left in the world.'

'Then she should be looking after the poor little mite,' Lil said crossly. 'She asks you for help one minute and the next she slopes off like a criminal. What's Matthew doing sending strangers to our door anyway?'

'She's obviously not a stranger to him, is she?' Tessa said flatly.

Weary to her bones now, and with no confidence that Iris would return, she wanted only to take to her bed, to close her eyes and put an end to this horrible day.

'Ex-WAAF, do you think?' Lil pondered, as she finished looking over the stock. 'Their paths must have crossed at some point.'

'I don't know.' Impatiently, Tessa's hand hovered by the gas lamp. 'Are you done yet, Lil? There's nothing missing.' Lil closed the till firmly.

'Not even a penny short. By the looks of it the stock's not been touched.' She shook her head in disbelief. 'You'd think she'd at least pinch a scarf to wrap that babby in.'

'She wasn't here to rob us.' Tessa sighed, turning off the lamp and plunging the shop back into darkness.

'All the same, get that door locked again,' Lil warned. 'We don't want all and sundry with their fingers in the till.'

She'd just take one last look out on to the street, Tessa decided. Just in case Iris was hiding in the shadows, wary of setting foot beyond them while she could still see Lil poking around the shop.

The lamp was off now and Lil had gone up to bed. If Iris regretted the sudden panic that had made her flee, perhaps the sight of Tessa alone in the darkness might persuade her to trust her as she obviously wished to.

But there was no sign of her. For a moment Tessa stood in the middle of Hockley Street, peering desperately in every direction, but it seemed that Iris Phelps, and her child, were long gone. Though a little warmer than when they arrived.

It was only when Tessa had locked the door once more and was hanging up her keys that she noticed the empty hook besides them.

Lil had turned the shop upside-down, but neither she nor Tessa had thought to check the hallway.

Tessa's mother's coat, the one thing she had left of her, was missing.

'You're not to go blaming yourself,' Dorrie told her firmly the next morning, when they were sitting either side of the counter stitching satin gloves.

'There's no sense in it, Tess. What's done is done.'

'Lil reckons I've seen the last of it,' Tessa confided. 'That coat was all I had left of my mum, Dorrie.'

'Only thing she left you, granted,' Dorrie said. 'But you've a whole lot more than that, Tess. You've your ma's talent, plain as the nose on your face. There's none can steal that away from you.'

Tessa managed a thin smile.

'I'd like my coat back all the same.'

'A Tessa Thorne original, that,' Dorrie reflected. 'Only one of its kind ever made. Might have been a different story if your ma and I had scrimped enough to set up our own shop, mind.'

'I think she'd like that you're helping me,' Tessa said.

She'd heard this tale so often, how as young women her mother and Dorrie had similar dreams to her own, the fancy they'd had for buying their passage on a ship to Paris where they'd start a boutique and sell Tessa Thorne originals, but she never tired of hearing it.

'All hands to the wheel if yesterday's anything to go by.' Dorrie smiled at her. 'More customers than we've seen in weeks, all after something pretty for when their husbands get home. We saw a fair few chaps as well, in civvies now but you can tell ex-services clear enough, all blowing their last pay packets on a little something for the missus. End of the war's got folk in a spending mood, Tess.'

'I was hoping it might.' One pair of gloves intricately stitched, Tessa reached for another. 'If I have to wait for my own husband, at least I can profit from everyone else's.'

'He'll be home soon, love.' Briefly Dorrie rested a comforting hand on Tessa's arm. 'Maybe he'll know where to find this Iris, get your coat back. Did she not say how she knows Matthew?'

Tessa shook her head.

'She looked knocked for six that I'd not heard of her.'

'Ex-air force, perhaps?' Dorrie suggested. 'Been discharged, fell on hard times and needing a friend.'

'That's what Lil said,' Tessa pondered. 'I just wish I knew why Matthew's kept quiet about her. He tells me everything, Dorrie.'

'Then he'll have his reasons, won't he? You know you can trust that man of yours, Tess.'

'I do trust him. I just wonder.'

'Wondering's not getting these gloves stitched now, is it?' Dorrie grinned at her as with infinite care she rested a finished pair into a tissue-lined box ready for sale. 'Time for a cuppa, Tess. I'll stick the kettle on, shall I?'

Working her fingers to the bone to meet specific orders as well as to stock the shelves in anticipation of this sudden clamouring for pretty Tessa Lane originals, the day Tessa had planned to spend on a train escorting Victoria back from Wales, she spent instead on a chair behind the counter, her sewing-machine only quietening for a few moments when a customer walked through the door.

Confined to the shop, she was not at liberty to traipse the streets looking for Iris Phelps.

In the meantime she'd be in the shop all day today. Maybe Iris might just pop back through the door. Unlikely, given the constant presence of either Lil or Dorrie as they took it in turns to look after the children, and the steadily increasing numbers of customers as the day went on, but there was always a chance.

Tessa had written to Matthew the night before. She'd fought exhaustion and scribbled by candlelight until her eyes were gritty and sore.

She'd told him everything. Victoria, Iris, how she'd let him down with both of them, but she'd not felt better for getting it off her chest. Usually she'd tell him everything that was troubling her. and feel purged by the end of it, as if he'd been sitting next to her the whole time and he'd squeezed her hand and told her not to be daft, like he always used to when she fretted over stuff.

She'd not taken that comfort from it this time. She'd not even posted the letter. Very rarely did letters to Matthew remain in her desk drawer for this long — usually she'd have been out catching the first post, wanting her words to be in his head as soon as she could manage it.

Maybe it was just that she didn't want to disappoint him. Once he read it he'd know she'd not only left his niece miles away from home, but she'd not helped his friend the way he'd trusted her to.

Every day she and Matthew were kept apart was another day the image of her in his head might be growing a little hazier.

When the rest of the country had been dancing in the streets to celebrate victory in Europe, Matthew had preferred to spend his stand-down from duty drinking and playing cards with his squadron. He'd chosen not to see her. When he was finally discharged from the air force, she wanted him to come straight home, to want to see her so much that however he got there it wouldn't be quick enough.

She didn't want their reunion to be blighted by blame and remorse.

She wanted to tell him everything when he was there by her side, when he could squeeze her hand and tell her not to be daft.

Come clocking-off time at Ambrose's, Tessa was always first out the gates; she'd started to make a habit of it. With one eye on the clock, soon as the bell rang for end of shift she was ready, sewing-machine stilled and the new coat she'd run up for herself thrown around her shoulders. It was nothing fancy, just a bit of material with sleeves, really, not her usual standard, but it was just for her so it didn't matter, and just to wear in the meantime, just until Iris Phelps returned her old one.

'Not the point,' Lil had protested. 'You're a walking advert for Li'l Tessa's — do our reputation no good if the whole of Brum sees you sporting any old rag.'

It was for Lil's sake that she was dashing home from the factory every day, barely holding herself back from barging past the gaggles of women who it seemed had nothing better to do than gather at the gates and talk for England. Tessa had a business to get back to, and orders to fill, and though she did as she'd always done, working her fingers to the bone until the early hours to keep up with it all, it was more the thought of Lil left holding the fort while she was at the factory that always had her breaking into a run.

Lil was delicate still, her nerves on edge, what with Anne and the new baby, and the shop on top of that, and to make matters worse, Bea, her sister-in-law, had been served her discharge papers and she was expected back in Brum any day now.

'Good old Auntie Bea,' Lil had muttered when Dorrie had imparted the news, her face glowing with happiness. 'Hero of the hour, she is. Just in time to ride to the rescue while Mummy slumps in a corner and drinks tea.'

While Tessa was at the factory, Lil and Dorrie manned the shop between them, taking it in turns to look after Anne and Victor. Small blessing they'd not be in the same room then, Tessa thought wryly. Dorrie was full of her daughter's impending return, her Bea, shining star of the Women's Air Force, and it would do Lil no good to hear constantly how brave and brilliant her sister-in-law was, not when Lil herself felt the exact opposite.

Having Victor had made no difference to her mood; bloated and uncomfortable she might no longer be, but Lil's spirits continued to dip and sour, and dip again.

'Motherhood,' Dorrie had confided in Tessa, 'can knock you for six no matter if it's your first or your twenty-first. Time to adjust to being a mother second time round, that's all she needs.'

Tessa had kept to herself the response that lingered temptingly on the tip of her tongue — that at least Lil and her babies had a roof over their head, and food in their bellies. It wouldn't do to compare her lot with anyone else's, no matter how favourably.

Every day Tessa looked out for Iris Phelps. Dashing home from Ambrose's, she always kept her eyes peeled. But it had been nearly a month now and she'd seen nothing more of her.

She'd not give up hope, though, Tessa vowed to herself. Whatever her reasons for taking fright and disappearing like that, Iris had needed help. In a moment of weakness she'd seen her chance and made off with Tessa's coat, but if her circumstances were as bad as Tessa suspected, she'd need a lot more than a coat to see her through.

Tessa had been down to the Housing Corporation, to ask after Iris, and as she'd expected they'd told her nothing, though from the blank expression on the clerk's face, she got the distinct impression it was not just a case of confidentiality, but genuinely nothing to tell.

Her letter to Matthew she'd eventually sent, as it was, all her thoughts unedited, and if he was disappointed in her then so be it. He loved her, nothing would change that. Besides, it felt unnatural to edit her words to Matthew; she'd be as well to write nothing at all if every letter was polite and stilted.

She'd yet to receive a reply, but she was choosing not to panic. In his last letter he'd told her a little of how he and his comrades were busy flying out supplies to liberated countries and bringing home freed prisoners. If the war in the East was drawing to a close she'd not bemoan a lack of letters, not if it meant he could get on with whatever he had left to do and come home to her all the sooner.

In the meantime business at Li'l Tessa's had picked up and, if it was only temporary before victory euphoria wore off and the economy slumped once more, it had yet to drop. Tessa knew she'd little chance of going from rags to riches overnight but the surge in sales had cheered her, at least.

Turning into Hockley Street now she noted with satisfaction a last trickle of customers descending the steps, their arms full of purchases, as Lil turned the sign. If this was anything to go by, it had been another fruitful day.

The downside to this was that Lil would be exhausted, no matter how much Dorrie had pitched in to help.

Tessa quickened her pace, hurrying up the steps and turning her key.

Lil always locked the door along with turning the sign; once she'd closed up she'd risk no more last-minute customers holding her up, no matter if it cost them the biggest sale of the day.

She was sitting behind the till, counting out profits, her face pale. She looked ready to drop with exhaustion. On the end of the counter sat Anne, swinging her legs to and fro as she played with cotton reels, threading them on to a length of wool, absorbed in her task. In the corner stood Victor's pram; and just as Tessa closed the door behind her, an almighty howl rose up from the depths of it.

'Where's Dorrie?' Tessa asked, as she rushed to scoop up Victor into her arms. 'Why have you got these two and the shop on your own?'

'Why shouldn't I have?' Lil demanded. 'I can't be a mother and a business-woman at once, you mean?'

'I don't mean anything of the sort, Lil, and you know I don't.' Tessa cradled Victor in her arms, and soothed now he had a shoulder to nestle into, he swiftly settled once more. 'It's just we're so busy at the minute, aren't we? Shop full of customers and these two rascals?' She aimed a smile at Anne, who grinned toothily back at her. 'Don't reckon I could manage it all day.'

'Of course you could. You're the great and super Auntie Tessa,' Lil muttered, but then the fight seemed to seep from her as she sagged on to a chair, sighing raggedly. 'Tess, I'm sorry. I've just been run off my feet.'

'So, where's Dorrie got to?'

'She's gone to the bank,' Lil informed her. 'All very hush-hush, as if she thinks for one minute I've got the energy to care. Oh, Anne! Now see what you've done!'

'It's all right, Lil, I'll see to it.' Tessa darted forward as Anne's collection of cotton reels clattered on to the floor. With Victor held firmly in one arm, with the other she lifted Anne down from the counter. 'You against me, young lady — whoever picks up the most wins, all right?'

Anne's lower lip had been trembling, her eyes watery as she watched Lil rest her head in her hands, but she smiled bravely, wiping the back of her sleeve across her face and sniffing determidly as she got to work scooping up cotton reels into the pocket of her dress.

Gently, Tessa lowered Victor back into his pram, holding her breath and letting it out again slowly when he didn't make a sound.

'He's off again,' she whispered. 'I'll finish up here, Lil. You get yourself upstairs and make a cup of tea.'

'No.' Lil shook her head firmly, but her eyes were a watery reflection of her daughter's as she gazed helplessly at Tessa. 'Will you take them out for a bit, Tess? Just for a walk round the block. I need five minutes to myself.'

'If that's what you need, of course I will.' Swooping down, Tessa grabbed the last cotton reel from the floor. 'Aha, young Miss Anne! I believe you might have won. Now your prize is a treasure hunt with your Auntie Tessa, so how about you fetch your coat while I get Victor all togged up?'

'Mummy's sad, isn't she?' Anne ventured moments later, as she walked along beside Tessa, one hand on Victor's pram and the other clutching Mary, her beloved doll. 'She gets cross with me all the time.'

Tessa chose her words carefully. Only four Anne may be, but she was a bright little thing. To fob her off with nothing would only serve to worry her more.

'Yes, poppet, Mummy's a little bit sad, but it's because she's very tired. That's why she gets cross sometimes.'

Anne thought about this, her little brow wrinkled in consternation.

'Why can't she just have a sleep then?' she wanted to know. 'When Victor cries because he's tired, Mummy puts him down for a sleep.'

'That's because Victor's just a baby,' Tessa explained. 'So he doesn't have any jobs to do. Mummy's busy in the day-time, isn't she?'

'Nanny helps,' Anne pointed out. 'And Daddy when he's not at work, and you, Auntie Tess. I help, too, don't I? Victor kept crying today so I let him have Rosie Rabbit in his pram for a bit.'

'That was kind of you.' Tessa squeezed the little girl's shoulders. 'You're a good big sister, Anne.'

'He likes Rosie Rabbit. He's not keeping her, though,' Anne added emphatically, and Tessa smiled to herself.

'No, indeed. Rosie belongs to you. Hold my hand while we cross the road, poppet.'

'Are we really going on a treasure hunt?' Anne asked eagerly, her green eyes shining with excitement as they rolled Victor's pram through the big iron gates into the park. 'Will we find real treasure? Like pirates, Auntie Tess?'

'Not quite the same as pirates,' Tessa told her. 'Because pirates keep their treasure and they don't share.'

'That's not very nice.' Anne wrinkled her nose in distaste. 'I want to share mine with Mummy,' she decided, and she raised an earnest face to Tessa. 'Can I, Auntie Tess? It'll make Mummy smile again if I give her treasure.'

Tessa felt her own eyes beginning to mist with tears as she smiled down at the little girl, but she blinked them back.

110

'Of course you can. You're right, Anne. Mummy would love some treasure.' Conspiratorially, she crouched down to whisper into her ear. 'And it just so happens that we've come to exactly the right place.'

'Can Mary help?' Anne held up her doll expectantly. 'She promises to behave.'

'As long as she's good.' Tessa eyed Mary mock sternly, making Anne giggle. 'No jumping in the lake or eating all the flowers, young Mary.'

The idea of a treasure hunt had just popped into her head at the last minute, but it had been a winning idea all the same, Tessa thought, as she watched Anne solemnly searching for a four-leafed clover, her faithful sidekick, Mary, tucked under her arm. A circuit of the park and they'd have collected all manner of treasure, and if it didn't bring an instant smile to Lil's face that her daughter had so devotedly sought out the prettiest flowers for her, then the treasure would be the smile on Anne's face that she'd done something so lovely

111

to cheer up her mother.

'Found one! I counted three times just in case!'

Anne bounded up to Victor's pram, the precious clover held lovingly in her palm.

'Good work, Miss Cooper.' Tessa bent to whisper into her ear once more. 'I spy a patch of bluebells over there. Do you know what bluebells mean?'

Anne shook her head, making her curls bob. 'Constancy,' Tessa told her.

'What's con . . . cons . . . what's that?'

'Constancy. It means always being there, and being patient and brave.' Tessa smiled at her. 'Your Mummy would like a bluebell, don't you think?'

Anne nodded, and bounded off to choose one.

As Victor began to stir, Tessa pushed the pram back and forth in a gentle rhythm, her thoughts drifting as she looked upon the distant sweep of the Lickey Hills.

They'd caught a tram out there, she and Matthew, just before he went off to join the air force, and they'd had a perfect day, walking and holding hands, sometimes talking, sometimes with no need for words. There was a big patch of bluebells by the lake there, they grew every year no matter what, and Matthew had picked just one of them and presented it to Tessa.

'For my beautiful and brave best friend,' he'd told her.

It had lived just a day or two, that bluebell. She'd put it straight in water, but before long its petals had started to droop. In the end she'd pressed it and she had it still, stowed away between the pages of her diary, and tucked away in her drawer with the lucky penny Victoria had found on the day of their wedding and solemnly presented to Tessa. She'd meant it to keep Matthew safe, and she'd believed in it, so Tessa had to, and she'd kept it all these years.

Matthew had made it this far, and he'd be home with her soon. She just wished every minute she had to wait didn't feel like an absolute lifetime.

'I found a pretty one.' Anne reached into her pocket and carefully withdrew the bluebell to show her. 'See?'

'That's definitely the prettiest of the whole patch.' Noting the second flower in Anne's hand, Tessa added, 'Is that one for Mary?'

Anne shook her head and smiled.

'Hold your hand out, Auntie Tess. It's for you,' she explained. 'To make you brave while you're waiting for Uncle Matthew to come home.'

This time she couldn't stop her eyes watering quick enough, and a solitary tear escaped and rolled down her cheek, much to Anne's dismay.

'Oh, no,' she murmured. 'Are you sad, too?'

'No, Anne, I'm not sad.' Tessa put an arm around her shoulders. 'Sometimes grown-ups cry happy tears.'

Anne frowned at her.

'I think that's a bit daft,' she decided. 'What's next to find, Auntie Tess?'

Having sent Anne scampering off to find a bird feather, Tessa placed the bluebell carefully into her handbag. She'd press this one, too, and put it with the other one.

Straightening again, she checked Anne was all right before her attention was taken up with Victor. It seemed he'd decided it was time to wake up, and he'd no intention of being rocked back to sleep.

'All right, then, young man,' Tessa told him. 'We shall have a nice stroll together while your sister finishes collecting her treasure.'

Scooping him up into her arms, she pulled his shawl tightly around him, taking care to keep him warm, as she did so her thoughts inevitably drifting to Iris Phelps and her child. At least they'd be warm, she thought wryly. That coat of her mother's was thick wool.

It was at that very moment she saw them. A passing glimpse; she blinked and they'd gone again, disappeared around a corner, but it had been them, she was sure of it almost as if she'd conjured them up from her thoughts.

Iris Phelps and her son.

'Least you know she's still around then,' Bertie said later, as he and Tessa sat by the fire with a cup of tea and a biscuit. 'Was she wearing your ma's coat?'

Tessa nodded.

'We chased after her but she'd disappeared again.'

'She'll show up when she's ready,' Bertie decided. 'And if she don't, Matthew might have an idea where to look.' He smiled at Tessa. 'Thank you, Tess. Our Anne were that excited she'd unearthed a whole hoard of treasure for her mum. You're a genius.'

'Wouldn't go that far,' Tessa said. 'Think Lil liked it though. I'm glad it made her smile for Anne's sake if nothing else.'

Bertie nodded, his expression solemn again.

'Tell me again how you found her, Tess.'

'She was sitting where we'd left her, in the shop, by the till, but she'd switched the wireless on.' Tessa smiled to herself remembering. 'They were playing one of her songs, one of her regulars from the Black Horse, and she was just listening, and smiling. It was like she was entranced, Bertie.' She looked up at him. 'It was like she was starting to wake up.'

Painting on a Smile

'Anyone would think we were feeding the whole air force,' Lil grumbled, as she cracked hard-boiled eggs into a bowl. Are you keeping an eye on them cakes, Tess? We'll be for it if they turn to cinders.'

'I've just this minute checked them.' Tessa peeled off the oven mitts and took up a knife to resume chopping salad. 'I know it seems Dorrie's gone a bit overboard on this, Lil. It's because Bea's been away so long, and they were always close, see.'

'That'll be why she's gone to meet her off the train, will it?' Lil looked at her pointedly. 'You'd think a woman who'd served her country for six years could find her way home without her ma to hold her hand.'

'She just wants to be there to meet her,' Tessa explained. 'Same as I will when Matthew comes home.'

'Bit different, though, Tess.' Lil reached

for a fork to begin mashing the eggs. 'You heard from him yet?'

'Letter came this morning.' Tessa kept her tone deceptively light as she concentrated on slicing radishes. 'He's safe and well,' she added quickly, hoping she'd avert any further questioning from Lil.

She knew well enough that if Lil had been her normal self, sharp as sixpence, she'd never have let Tessa get away with being so vague, but Lil wasn't herself, not just yet. The treasure Anne had collected sat proudly in a bowl on her bedside table, and there'd been more times since when she'd sat with a dreamy look on her face, listening to a favomite tune on the wireless, but she still had moments when it was all she could do to raise a smile.

'He'll be the next one home,' she assured Tessa. 'And I shan't mind how many eggs I mash up for your Matthew.'

Tessa smiled thinly.

He'd written to her, finally. It'd been a while, but she already knew how busy he was flying supplies out one way and bringing soldiers back the other, so she'd not worried too much. She'd kept writing to him anyway, because she knew he relied on her to keep him going, to make him feel he wasn't really all that far away.

So he'd have known everything when he'd put pen to paper this time.

He'd have known that Victoria was still living with Granny Peg, and he'd have known that Tessa had yet to cross paths with Iris Phelps. She knew he'd received that first letter that explained it all, because in it she'd also told him other things, about the shop, Lil and the children, and he'd responded to these in his reply. But of Victoria or Iris he'd made no mention.

Not a word had he written of either of them, not even to reassure Tessa it didn't matter, that he didn't despise her for getting it wrong, and he'd know she'd be fretting over it because he knew her so well.

There was only one possible conclusion to reach, Tessa thought sadly.

Matthew was angry and hurt by her

actions, and he couldn't find the words to put it in a letter. He was waiting until he saw her, until he could look her in the eye and ask her why she'd let him down so badly.

'Where's Bertie got to?' she asked Lil as brightly as she could. It wouldn't do to dwell on everything, not today. Bea deserved a bit of a fuss made of her.

'Rolling out the red carpet,' Lil muttered, as she began to spread thickly buttered bread with chopped up egg. 'I don't know. He said he had stuff to do. Might have took Victor with him. His Lordship wakes up now, the grand feast will have to wait five minutes.'

Tessa glanced over at the baby basket, where Victor was sleeping soundly.

'He's fast asleep, Lil. But if he does wake up, I'll finish off here. Anne's gone with Dorrie, has she?'

'All dolled up in her prettiest frock and gone to welcome Auntie Bea, yes.' Lil laid down her knife a moment, wiping her hands on a tea towel as she grabbed the kettle and crossed to the sink to fill it. 'Banquet can wait. I need a cuppa. Tess?'

'Go on, then. Suppose I'd better check those cakes.'

It would be nice to see Bea again, Tessa thought. They'd always been friends, she and Bea, from when they were little and playing in Dorrie's backyard. She was looking forward to chatting with her old friend. She felt somehow that it brought Matthew a little closer, not just because Bea could tell her tales of life in the air force, but also because Bea could remember a time when they were all safely here in Birmingham, when Matthew wasn't off flying planes over dangerous territory.

Bea was her friend, pure and simple, and of course it was a relief to have her home safe and sound. Not that she'd been without a close female friend in the meantime; Lil had filled Bea's shoes more than adequately.

Poor Lil, feeling like she was about to be cast aside, what with Dorrie glowing over the return of her daughter, Anne insisting she dress Mary up in her Sunday best to go meet Bea off the train, and here was Tessa looking forward to a good old chinwag with her old friend as if she'd had no shoulder to cry on for the past six years.

And goodness only knew where Bertie had gone, and what he was up to. Not a good time to be all mysterious, Tessa thought wryly, not with Lil's nerves on edge at the imminent return of Dorrie's favoured daughter.

Leaving the salad for a minute, Tessa went to reach an arm around Lil's shoulders.

'What's that for?' Lil looked at her, surprised.

'You're my friend,' Tessa said simply. 'It'll all be all right, Lil, you know.'

'Will it?' But for a brief moment Lil rested her head on Tessa's shoulder. 'Might want to tell yourself that, Tess,' she munnured. 'Or was there something in that letter from Matthew that's got your face looking like a wet weekend?'

'I just miss him, that's all,' Tessa said

quickly. It wasn't a lie, but then neither was it the whole truth.

She wasn't all that sure why she'd balked at telling Lil the rest of it, especially when she'd not even expected her to notice anything was wrong, and yet here was Lil, brewing up a pot of tea and clearing a space on the table for the biscuit tin, ready with a listening ear, but Tessa kept her mouth clamped shut.

Guilt maybe, she reasoned. She'd done wrong by Matthew and she was that ashamed of it she didn't even want to unburden herself to her good friend Lil. Or perhaps she just didn't want to put it into words and make it real.

'Mithering over something, you are,' Lil observed, watching her closely as she sipped her tea. 'But maybe you're saving it for when Bea's here to lend you a shoulder.'

'Don't be daft.' Tessa managed a smile. 'I miss him, Lil, and I suppose I just feel I've failed him a bit, you know, by not bringing Victoria home,' she added lamely, stopping short of telling her the rest of it.

Lil raised an eyebrow at her.

'Did he say that? He'll be getting the sharp edge of my tongue if he breathes a word about it, Tess. If it weren't for you, he'd have no home and no living to come back to now, would he? All very well flying high in that squadron of his, but how many ribbons he's got stitched on his tunic will mean nothing back in Civvy Street.' She rummaged in the biscuit tin, seeking out the ginger ones. 'As for Miss Victoria, she wants to count herself lucky she's got an aunt who gives two hoots about her. Not long to go now, is there? Before school finishes for the summer?'

'A month or so,' Tessa told her. 'Soon as she's done I'll go back and get her.'

She sounded far more confident than she felt, she thought, feeling her insides twist at the prospect. What if Victoria refused to come back with her all over again? What if Granny Peg sided with her? Tessa could hardly drag her kicking and screaming to the station. Maybe Matthew would be home in time; maybe he could go and fetch her instead. He'd want to go anyway, she realised. He'd not trust Tessa to do it now.

* * *

'Ever so lovely, this is!' Bea Cooper exclaimed. 'You needn't have gone to so much trouble, not just for me.'

'Not every day my only daughter comes home after six years defending us all,' Dorrie stated proudly. 'Bit of a spread's the least you deserve, love.'

'Listening to her, you'd think our Bea had won the war single-handedly,' Bertie quipped. 'Don't know what the rest of 'em were playing about at then. What's Matthew been doing these past six years, Tess? Playing cards and making tea?'

Bea had been home five minutes, and she'd not had time to catch her breath before Dorrie had been on at her, wanting to hear all about it, as if she'd come back from a week at the seaside, not six years helping to fight a war, Tessa thought wryly.

She'd done them proud, though; quiet, unassuming little Bea Cooper, who'd learned to be a dab hand at detecting enemy aircraft and kept her head about it even when there'd been bombs dropped on the base and she'd lost three of her friends in one go, but Bea had lived to tell the tale. Only to be expected Dorrie would want to make a fuss of her. Bea had made it home. There were a fair few who hadn't.

'You look done in, Bea,' Lil observed. 'Dorrie's made you up the spare room next to Tessa's if you want to get your head down for a bit.'

'Plenty of time for that later,' Dorrie chipped in, a little irritably. 'She's not seen us for months, Lil. Let her have a cuppa and a bit of a chat before you pack her off to bed.'

Bea had missed them, all right — her eyes had watered a bit when she'd done the round of welcome-back embraces — but then she'd sunk into an armchair and not moved since, chatting occasionally, but for the most part happy to sit with her cup of tea and let her mother do the talking.

They'd be lucky, the rest of them, if they managed to get a word in, but then no-one seemed to have that much to say. Bea was so tired out her eyes began to glaze over the longer she sat there, Lil was on edge at the return of Dorrie's daughter, even the ever-cheerful Bertie seemed a bit at odds over it all, and as for Tessa, all she could think about was Matthew, if he'd be home soon, if Bea's safe return meant she'd no right to expect another, not when there were so many families she knew of hereabouts who'd had the telegram and so wouldn't be expecting anyone.

'You've timed this just right, Bea!' Dorrie exclaimed brightly, as if the matter of Bea's release from the WAAF had been her own doing. 'Li'l Tessa's has a big order of frocks to see to, and you've always had a knack with a sewing-machine. You help out while Tessa's at the factory and it'll take the work off Lil's shoulders, free up her time for the children.'

'Might want to let her finish her cuppa before you plonk her back in front of a sewing-machine, Ma,' Bertie chided her, keeping his tone light, but Tessa saw the hand he placed reassuringly on to Lil's shoulder. 'She's only been back here five minutes.'

'Do her good to get back to normal, won't it, love?' Dorrie reached across to pat Bea's arm fondly. 'Sewing always was your thing, you and Tess. Just like her ma and me in our day, you were.' She smiled to herself.

'Shall we have a bit of a tune?' Bertie leapt up and crossed to the mantel shelf, one eye still on Lil as he fiddled with the dial on the wireless.

'Smashing,' he declared, when the perfect tune for a waltz filled the silence, and he held out a hand to Lil. 'Dance with me, Mrs Cooper?'

Lil got quickly to her feet, but she'd no intention of being waltzed around the room.

'About time I looked in on Victor,' she

said flatly. 'Get your Bea up and dancing, or Tessa, or your mother. I'm not in the mood, Bertie.'

Like a puppet on a string, pulled up sharp, Anne's head shot up, her green eyes fixed on to Lil.

'Mummy, are you sad again?'

Lil swallowed hard, blinking back tears.

'No, love, Mummy's not sad. Mummy's just a bit too tired to dance.'

It was for Anne's sake Lil allowed herself to be persuaded back into the armchair, Tessa noticed, watching how she beckoned to her daughter, pulling her up on to her lap and holding her tight.

Anne nestled into Lil's shoulder, Mary the doll and Rosie Rabbit lying forgotten on the hearth rug. Four years old and all grown up she might be, but Anne needed to be held, needed reassuring that Mummy wouldn't be sad for ever.

'Fine pair of lungs your nephew's got on him, Bea,' Dorrie spoke, competing with the crackle of the wireless to fill the sudden silence. 'Whole street will know the minute he opens his eyes.'

'Takes after his pa then,' Bea said, a little of the old twinkle in her eye. 'Far too much to say for himself.'

Perched once more on the arm of his wife's chair, Bertie smiled down at her.

'No, he takes after his mum. He'll be singing before he can read, will our Victor.'

'Not if I have anything to say about it, he won't.' Mindful of Anne cuddled up on her lap, Lil did her best to keep her tone light, but Tessa heard the tenacity, the sheer grit behind her words, and when she looked at Bertie's face she knew he'd heard it, too.

He'd not bring up the whole singing thing now, not while they had an audience. He'd challenge her about it later, when it was just the two of them.

Bertie Cooper would cut out his own tongue before he said one word to knowingly offend his Lil.

She was lucky her gran wasn't here, Tessa thought wryly. Granny Peg knew best of them all how a love of singing was in Lil's blood, as much a part of her as the hair on her head, and she'd make no bones about it. Lil should be getting herself down the Black Horse of a Saturday afternoon, and she'd feel a ton lighter, soon as she opened her mouth.

It was perhaps because Bertie knew it, too, that, this time, he kept talking.

'This morning, when I said I'd stuff to see to,' he began, turning in towards Lil, 'I were down the Black Horse, having a word with Jeannie.'

'I wondered where you'd got to,' Lil rebuked him mildly. 'There's me making sandwiches and watching our son, while you're off sharing a jar with the pub landlady.'

'He were polishing that piano of his, more like,' Bea piped up, and Bertie whipped round to give her a look, cross that she'd interrupted.

'Actually I'll be running a duster over it soon as I've a minute, and it's partly down to you gracing us with your presence again.' Turning back towards Lil, he picked up one of her hands and held it in his for all the world like it was a precious jewel. 'I thought it might be a good time to put on a bit of a sing-song, celebrate the end of the war the way we do best, me on the piano and you at my side,' he added, less sure of himself when he caught the look on Lil's face. 'I miss that, Lil. I miss us, performing together.'

It seemed to Tessa that the whole room went quiet waiting to hear Lil's response. Even the wireless sounded all muffled and Dorrie got up to go and fiddle with the dial, but her eyes were on her daughter-in-law.

'So what's Jeannie's take on this big idea of yours?' Lil asked Bertie. 'Planning on filling the place, is she? Cheap ale and streamers draped over anything that don't move?'

'She knows she'll be on to a winner soon as she puts up posters with your name splashed across 'em,' Bertie declared. 'It's been too long, Lil. Every Saturday when I'm down there playing to a half-empty room, there's a fair few regulars clamouring to hear you sing, and I'm telling you now there'll be a fair few more filling the place once word gets round that you're making an appearance.'

'Appearing I've got no problem with,' Lil told him, a sharp edge returning to her voice. 'But if you're expecting me to get up there and sing you'll be disappointed.'

Bertie's face crumpled.

'Without you we've no show,' he said flatly, but Lil just shrugged as she got to her feet, Anne held tight in her arms.

'Then you've no show. You'd best get back down there and give Jeannie the bad news. I'll see to Victor,' she added, as with perfect timing their son announced the end of his nap with a piercing wail.

With not so much as a glance at any of them, Lil made her escape, taking Anne with her, and leaving a defeated Bertie slumped in the chair.

'You know what your Lil's like once she digs her heels in,' Dorrie cautioned him once the bedroom door had slammed and Lil was out of earshot. 'I think you'd be best to tell Jeannie it's all off. Wouldn't do to keep her thinking she's got a show to promote.'

Bertie's expression was cold as he looked up at his mother.

'I'm telling her nothing of the sort. Good job Lil has more of us than just you to believe in her, isn't it?'

'She did sound like she'd no intention of singing a note, Bertie.' Bea spoke up in defence of her mother, earning herself a withering look from Bertie.

'You don't know my Lil well enough to say, Bea. Nor do you know what it is to be part of a marriage, to take the good with the bad, to know which battles to pick.' He shook his head in disbelief. 'War heroine you might be, but back here you're six years behind the rest of us.' To illustrate his point, Bertie turned instead to Tessa, the one who did understand, and his tone was friendlier. 'Will you go talk to her, Tess? She'll listen to you.'

'I'll see she's all right,' Tessa corrected

him.

Tessa glanced quickly across at Bea before she got to her feet. Bea had been knocked for six by her brother's harsh words, but then Bea had Dorrie who flew to her side like a mother hen.

Bea she'd talk to later. For now Lil needed her more. 'Sent you to talk me into it?' Lil spared Tessa a cursory glance, her arms full of a wriggling Victor. Once she'd got the bottle in his mouth and he was settled on her lap, she looked back at her. 'What's he doing telling Jeannie I'll get up and sing before he's even said a word to me about it?'

'His way of helping you back through the door, maybe?' Tessa chose her words carefully. She'd not gone in there to plead Bertie's case for him, but Lil clearly wanted to talk about it. 'He knows you love singing.'

'So he's after tricking me into it?' Lil interrupted, but the anger had gone, fizzled like a candle flame in a gust of wind, and she spoke in a whisper, sounding sad and hopeless, her head bowed as if she was ashamed to look Tessa in the eye. 'I can't, Tess. I can't do it.'

Tessa looked across at Anne. She was sitting on the ottoman, swinging her legs to and fro; in one hand she clutched Lil's hand-held mirror, absorbed in her reflection as she wound her brown curls around her fingers.

But she'd be listening still; she'd have caught every word.

'Oh, my, who is that beautiful young lady in the mirror?' Tessa sat beside her on the ottoman, and Anne looked at her with the endless patience of a child humouring the grown-up.

'It's me, Auntie Tess.'

'So it is.' Tessa whipped out from behind her back the doll she'd grabbed from the hearth rug. 'Poor old Mary feels like Cinderella, all rags and nowhere to go. Tell you what . . .' She stood up, lifting Anne up into her anus. 'I think you should get her ready for the ball. Comb her hair for her, and let's get those ribbons tidy.'

'Use Mummy's hairbrush,' Lil added.

'And Mary might like a pretty brooch to wear, do you think, Anne? Ask Auntie Tess to open my jewellery box and you have a rummage, but be careful with those brooch pins, we don't want Mary with holes in her, do we?'

Anne knelt on the stool in front of the dressing table, carefully propping Mary up against the mirror while Tessa undid the clasp on Lil's jewellery box.

She'd be content enough, dolling Mary up to look like a princess, even if she knew all the same that Mummy was talking in her sad voice to Auntie Tess.

Better this way than banishing her to the front room with Daddy and Nanny and Aunty Bea — she'd just fret all the more then.

Lil looked a bit calmer. She managed a tired smile when Tessa returned to sit beside her on the edge of her bed.

'Thanks, Tess. You've a way with our Anne. She thinks the world of you.' She hesitated. 'Be a good mum, you will, when the time comes.'

Tessa nodded, managing a smile in

return.

'Matthew and me, we've not talked about children.'

'You've not had chance to,' Lil returned bluntly. 'Married one minute, him running off to fly Spits the next, and any time you've had, well, I don't suppose you'll have been thinking all that much about the future, not when every minute of the present's had to count.'

It had counted, every minute had counted, few and precious as they were. And Lil was wrong, though she'd not tell her that. She and Matthew had talked a bit about after the war, where they'd be and what they'd do, but he'd never wanted to go too much into it, now she thought about it, he'd always stopped short of promising her anything.

She knew why, of course she did. He'd spent the past six years knowing there was a chance he could be killed at any minute. Same as they all had. But Matthew had been up there, flying headlong into swarms of enemy planes, dodging bullet fire with the luck of the devil.

Even when he'd been transferred to Wales, out of active service while he instructed new pilot's, Hawarden air base had been no less dangerous than any other, a sitting target for the enemy who was intent on blowing up the lot.

He'd seen a good many comrades shot down, Matthew had. Not that he talked much about that either. He couldn't. When he was with Tessa he just wanted it to be them, no ghosts playing gooseberry.

It'd do him good, Tessa thought, to get on with his life. It'd do them both good. No sense in dwelling on the war, the people they'd lost. It wouldn't be healthy for Victoria, for a start.

Tessa wanted a proper marriage, to live with her best friend for the rest of her life. She wanted to have children with Matthew. She wanted what Lil and Bertie had.

'Stick that on the table, Tess.' Lil handed her Victor's empty bottle, shifting him up on to her shoulder. 'Anne all right, is she?'

140

Anne swivelled round to grin at her.

'I'm all right, Mummy. But Mary thinks Victor sounds like a piglet when he sucks his bottle.'

'Mary's quite right.' Lil rubbed circles on Victor's back. 'A little piglet he most certainly is.'

Tessa caught her eye and smiled at her.

'Takes one to know one — a good mum, I mean, not a piglet,' she added. 'You'll be no less of a mother if you spend an hour singing to the regulars every Saturday, Lil.'

She'd take a chance and push this a bit further, she thought. The look in Lil's eyes was the one she'd got quite a bit just lately, all sad and wistful.

'Your gran was telling me how, when you were a babby, you used to sleep in the back room of the pub while your mother was singing to the crowds,' she continued. 'There's plenty of us to watch Victor, and as for Anne, I reckon she'd think it was smashing.'

Lil shook her head, but there was a

yearning in her eyes she couldn't quite conceal.

'I can't, Tess.'

'What was it they used to say?' Tessa reminded her gently: 'Voice of an angel, that Lillian Cooper's got. Our very own Gracie Fields right here in Brum.' She squeezed Lil's hand. 'And you loved every minute of it. What's stopping you now?'

Lil's voice trembled as she whispered.

'My mum. When I sing, every note makes me think of her, and I can see her, clear as if we're back in Gran's house, gathered round the piano of a Saturday afternoon, me and mum and Aunty Mai, and now there's only me left.'

'Don't you think she'd be proud of you?'

She smiled sadly, settling a newly winded Victor on to her lap and reaching for his rattle.

'I know she would. She was. When I sang to them her face was a picture. But I'm more than that now, Tess. I'm a mother. I've got these two.'

'Reckon she'd be proud of you for that as well.'

She'd hit the nail on the head, Tessa thought. Soon as the words were out of her mouth, she knew. The look on Lil's face said it all.

'But she'll never know them, will she? She'll never know her grandchildren.' She gazed helplessly at Tessa, the tears finally rolling slowly down her cheeks. 'I feel like my heart's breaking, Tess. How am I supposed to sing?'

★ ★ ★

Bertie sat on the carpet, one arm steadying his son, who chuckled to himself as he beat his rattle on the floor like a drum. Downstairs Dorrie's ears would be ringing as she held the fort, showing Bea around Li'l Tessa's with as much pride as if it had been hers all along.

Tessa had dragged the ottoman to stand beside the stool, so that she, Lil and Anne could sit in a row at the dressing table. Like blackbirds perched on a branch, she'd told Anne, who'd grinned delightedly at the image. She and Mummy and Auntie Tess, getting all dolled up like Cinderella, and not because they'd be going to the ball — Mummy hadn't made her mind up yet — but just because Auntie Tess knew it would make Mummy feel a little bit better if she had her hair done up all pretty and put a bit of lipstick on. Mummy used to be a proper Cinderella, Auntie Tess had told her.

Anne thought that Mummy still was.

In the mirror Lil's reflection smiled gratefully at Tessa.

'Thank you,' she whispered.

We'll Sing Again . . .

Not since all the delirium of the VE Day celebrations had the Black Horse Inn looked such a picture, Tessa thought, pausing a moment up on the top rung of the stepladder to scrutinise her haniwork. She'd been down here since the end of her shift at the factory, lending Jeannie and Bertie a hand to get the place all scrubbed up and ready.

Jeannie had in the back all the flags and streamers she'd hung for VE Day, still in pretty good shape given how wild and raucous the dancing had got; she'd commented to Tessa, with arched eyebrows and a knowing grin.

Two minutes it had taken her to dig them out and Tessa had been up the stepladder with armfuls of red, white and blue, seeing to it that every corner was bedecked in victory colours.

'Should have left 'em up really, shouldn't I?' Jeannie pondered, passing beneath with polish and a duster. 'Mood folk are in, can't imagine it would have caused offence. Are you done up that ladder, Tess? Don't want broken bones to contend with tonight of all nights, thanks very much.'

'I'm all done' Tessa assured her, climbing back down to floor level.

'Ladder's to go back in the storeroom, is it?'

'Not yet. Bertie's banner wants hanging over the bar.' Jeannie looked up from the table she was polishing. 'It's out the back, Tess, but don't you be hangmg that on your own. I'll give you a hand once I'm done here.'

Tessa headed through to the back room, where she found the banner Bertie had made draped across the table.

One Night Only — Lillian Cooper and guests!

Jeannie had called in a few favours, twisted arms and badgered other singers into lending their time and talent for Bertie's peacetime knees-up, so it'd not just be Lil taking to the stage. He'd given her top billing, though, Tessa thought ruefully. Lil hadn't said one way or another, not for definite, but Bertie had gone ahead and put her up in lights anyway.

She'd not stopped him, so perhaps he'd been right to do it. Perhaps all she'd needed was a bit of a push.

Tessa had talked to him about it, told him how simple it was when it came down to it.

'She misses her mum, Bertie. Having Anne and Victor, it's brought it home to her just how much. And singing's what she did with her mum, so it's painful. But she's not lost that look she gets when she hears one of her favourite songs. Just give her time.'

'I'll give her all the time she wants.' Bertie had sighed. 'I'll burn my piano to the ground before I rush her into anything, but I hate seeing her this unhappy, Tess, and I know what it does for her; the music, the adoration, the feeling I know she gets that she could fly the second she starts to sing.' He'd smiled sadly, remembering. 'I want that for her. I want her to feel like that again, like she could soar.'

So he'd gone ahead and arranged it all, emblazoning her name across posters and the banner Anne had helped him to paint. Lil had seen it; she knew what he was up to, and she'd said nothing about it.

No news was good news, Tessa thought hopefully. Maybe Lil just needed a bit of time to reflect, to get used to the idea.

As for Bertie, he needed this to go without a hitch, and Tessa knew why, because she'd known Bertie far too long to be fooled by the smiles he always hid behind.

Bea coming back, and Dorrie making such a fuss of her, the daughter who'd bravely served her country for six years, it had made Bertie feel he had to prove himself. He was no war hero, though his job working for the gas board, a reserved occupation, had meant he'd done plenty here in Birmingham, making pipes safe after bombs had exploded, and helping to dig people out all over the place. Bertie had seen his fair share of pain and suffering, all right, but he wore no medals to prove it.

And now he couldn't seem to make his wife happy, either. Bertie needed to throw this party, and he needed Lil to remember how good they'd been together, him playing the piano while she rested a hand on his shoulder and sang like an angel.

He'd turned up by the time Tessa had carefully carried the banner through to the bar, and he was talking to Jeannie.

'Tess.' He looked up at her and smiled. 'Looks smashing in here, thanks. Give me a minute and I'll help you with that.'

'You want my duster and polish for that piano of yours, Bertie?' Jeannie teased him, and he grinned at her.

'Done it already. You can see your face in my piano.'

Jeannie went out to finish making up the sandwiches, leaving Bertie to help Tessa string up the banner.

'How's Lil feeling?' Tessa asked him. 'Has she said if she's coming down later?'

Bertie deposited the stepladder down

beneath the bar, squinting up at it thoughtfully.

'Reckon that will stretch nicely across, don't you?' He glanced at her. 'I don't know, Tess. She's not said one way or the other. But she'll not let me down, will she?' he added, more confident now as he climbed up to the top rung and reached down for one end of the banner. 'Here, pass it up, bit at a time. She knows I've promised folk a tune or two from Lillian Cooper, she'll not disappoint.'

'For your sake, then.' Tessa fed more of the banner up to him. 'I could have gone up and done this, Bertie.'

He sent a smile back down to her.

'I know. Surefooted as a cat, you are, Tessa. Thing is, I'd rather not have to tell Matthew his wife's in hospital after tumbling off the top of a ladder, if it's all the same to you.'

'He'd not hold it against you,' Tessa assured him. 'He knows me too well.'

'Heard anything more from him yet?' Bertie enquired. 'I know it's still all going on out East, but I reckon Matthew's done over and above his bit by now, Tess.'

She shook her head.

'Not a word about when he's coming home.'

Not a word about the rest of it, either, she thought. At last he'd made a passing reference to Victoria, writing that they'd fetch her home soon as he was back, but he'd said nothing of how he felt about Tessa just leaving her there with Granny Peg, and he'd still made no mention at all of Iris Phelps.

'It can't be long now, can it?' Bertie reasoned. 'I mean, Bea's been home best part of a month, hasn't she?'

'Don't mean anything, though,' Tessa said flatly. 'Bea said releases from the Forces are controlled to the letter, few at a time so they don't take all the jobs at once.'

'Well, our Bea won't be after one of them, will she?' Bertie exclaimed. 'Set up nicely in that shop of yours, she is.' Climbing down to the floor, he glanced pointedly at Tessa as he moved the step-ladder to the other end of the bar. 'Don't let Ma take over, Tess. She's too caught up in what might have been, you know, her and your ma and their little empire. It's your shop, yours and Lil's. It's your decision whether Bea gets her feet under the table or has to take herself off down the Labour Exchange like everyone else.'

'I don't mind Bea working in the shop,' Tessa conceded. 'Dorrie's right, it makes sense for her to lend a hand, what with all these big orders we're still getting, and me stuck in the factory five days a week. Lil doesn't seem to mind her being there.'

'Lil doesn't care, Tess.' Bertie climbed back to the top of the ladder, reaching down to take the other end of the banner. 'The shop's just a means of putting food on the table for her. You do know that, don't you?'

She knew it had always been her dream, not Lil's. Of course she knew. Lil had always said, 'You're the talent, Tess, we've no business without you', but without Lil, without her Aunty Mai's money, there'd have been no shop to set up the business in.

How many times had Tessa felt so deeply beholden to her, so guilty that it would be years yet before she could even think of paying her back?

But Lil hadn't pushed her on it, she'd seemed happy to have the shop ticking over, and to work in it herself; ever since she'd arrived in Birmingham six years ago and landed herself a job working with Tessa at Ambrose's, she'd known her way around a sewing-machine.

These days Lil was finding it hard to care much about anything besides the children, but not once had she said for definite she had no further interest in Li'l Tessa's.

Did she want to sell up and move on? Had she had enough of investing in Tessa's dream, especially given how up and down profits had been just lately?

'Pass me up another one of those tacks,' Bertie instructed. 'What's up with your face, Tessa Lane? It's a happy occasion tonight, smiles all round, if you please.'

'Sorry.' Tessa forced a smile. 'There. Happy now?'

'I will be if this looks halfway presentable. Hang on.' Bertie climbed down again, backing up and narrowing his eyes to squint at the banner.

'There,' he said, satisfied it looked all right. 'That'll do nicely. So what's got you looking all glum, apart from the usual?'

'How much I miss Matthew, you mean?' Tessa rubbed the pad of her thumb across a glass ring on the bar. 'That's the worst of it. But then I've got the worry of having a roof over his head when he does come back.'

Bertie looked momentarily confused as he folded the stepladder, but then recognition dawned.

'You're worried Lil wants to sell up.'

'Does she?'

He leaned on the ladder a minute eyeing her thoughtfully, debating how much to tell her, Tessa thought.

'Tell me, Bertie.'

He sighed.

'We've talked about it, Tess. It's nothing against you. Lil and me, we'll neither of us see you out on the street, you know that. It's just the shop, the whole business of clothing the city in Tessa Lane originals, it's your dream, Tess.'

'I know,' she finished flatly. 'It was never Lil's.'

Bertie rested a hand briefly on her shoulder.

'Nothing's set in stone, not yet. Way Lil's up and down at the minute, it's no time to be deciding anything for definite. But it seems to me we'd be best off putting everything right and be done with it.' He smiled at her.

'Got this concert to get through first, eh? My Lil, drawing in the crowds like she always did. That voice of hers, Tess, she don't really need me on the piano now, does she?'

'Of course she does.' Tessa managed a smile as he carried the stepladder past her, and through into the storeroom. 'She needs you by her side, Bertie.'

She'd not dwell on the chances of

losing her business, and the roof over her head, not tonight. While there was a chance Lil would sing, she'd just concentrate on being here to support her. Tonight it needed to be about Lil.

She'd save it for later, for when she was back in her bed, and when it was dark and quiet and nobody would see much less mind if she gave way to tears; only then would she think about it, only then would she wonder what in the world she was supposed to do if she lost her home and her dream in one fell swoop.

* * *

'Can't believe she's actually here, can you?' Bea leaned in towards Tessa, having to shout over the din to make herself heard. 'I'm telling you, Tess, right up until she walked out that door with me, I was convinced she were about to have second thoughts.'

'She'll not let Bertie down,' Tessa assured her. 'Dorrie's not bringing the children, then? I thought she might. Just for a bit, anyway, just so Anne could hear her mum get up and sing.'

'Lil asked her not to,' Bea said. 'Course, Ma weren't all that fussed. You know how she likes her time with her grandkids. She'd choose milk and biscuits over beer and a knees-up any day of the week!'

'Would have been nice for Anne to hear her mum sing, though.'

Bea shrugged.

'Lil wanted them to stay at home. Least she's here, I were half expecting her to stay there with them.'

There'd be other times, Tessa thought. Anne would have plenty of opportunities to hear her mum sing, to see how everyone loved her, how they listened as if entranced and then raised the roof with their clapping afterwards.

Once Lil had got up beside Bertie tonight and sang her heart out, and started to heal it while she was at it, she'd be back in the swing of her Saturday afternoons down the Black Horse.

It was perhaps for the best that she'd

wanted the children to stay at home this first time, while she was feeling a bit up in the air about it all. She knew Anne would see the way her stomach would be twisting itself in knots and she'd not want her to fret.

Nor would she want Anne to watch her climb on shaky legs up on to the makeshift stage, to stand beside Bertie's piano. She'd not want her to see the look in Bertie's eyes the instant he realised.

And she'd not want her to see the way she stood there for what felt like the longest moment and not sing a note.

'Go after her, Tess. Please.'

Bertie stood on the pavement outside the Black Horse, grim faced, watching Lil run off back down Gerard Street, near enough tripping over her own feet in her haste to get away from the pub, the impatient crowd, from the look on Bertie's face.

She'd had her coat half on, Tessa had, the minute she'd realised Lil wasn't going to sing, and she'd been up and pushing her way through the pub, packed like sardines though it was. She'd given no thought to Bea, left on her own and with a catcalling crowd to contend with, but then Bea had given no thought to Lil, had she?

Might be best that Bea had stopped in there, Tessa reasoned, as she took off after Lil. Bertie would need a bit of moral support when he went back in to finish his set. She couldn't imagine how he'd manage it, how he'd put on a brave face, but he'd find a way. Bertie always did.

Not all that far behind Lil, Tessa had caught up with her by the time they'd turned the corner at the end of Gerard Street.

'Lil, wait.'

With not even a glance back over her shoulder, Lil quickened her pace, hunching her shoulders as if to bury herself further down into her coat.

'Leave me alone, Tess.'

'Can't. I promised Bertie. And me — I promised me, too.' Tessa hesitated, then added gently, 'It's as black as coal out here, Lil. Can't we go home and have a cuppa?'

Lil slowed down a bit, though she kept her eyes fixed on the pavement.

'And what'll I tell Dorrie?' she asked, her voice all croaky. 'I've ruined her son's big night.'

'You've not ruined anything,' Tessa said quickly. 'Jeannie's got others lined up to sing, remember.'

'Doesn't matter. I've ruined Bertie's night.' At last Lil stopped in her tracks and turned to look at Tessa. Her face was ashen. 'I couldn't do it, Tess. I couldn't.'

'I know, love. I know you couldn't.'

'I'm sorry.' It was barely even a whisper.

'It's all right. Really it is. You weren't ready, Lil, that's all there is to it.' Gently, Tessa took Lil's arm and slipped it under her own. 'Come on, let's go home. There's not much that don't look better after a nice cup of tea.'

With a shuddering sigh that took the last scrap of energy she had, Lil leant heavily on Tessa's arm all the way back to Hockley Street. She'd nothing more to say about it, and Tessa decided she'd not push her to. Best thing for her now was a good, strong cup of tea, and then to bed for a decent sleep. There'd be plenty of time to talk about it tomorrow.

She'd take Dorrie to one side, Tessa decided; soon as they got in she'd have a quick word, so Dorrie would know not to keep on about it.

At least the children would be in bed by this hour; that was one thing to be thankful for. Just a baby Victor might have been, but he'd know the minute Lil held him. He was taking after his sister, picking up on Lil's moods as easily as cats picked up fleas. As for Anne, she'd helped Bertie paint the banner, and she'd been so excited that Mummy was going to get up on stage and sing like a film star; as soon as she saw Lil's face she'd understand it hadn't gone right, but she was so enchanted by the whole thing she'd want to hear all about it anyway, she'd not be able to stop herself.

Good thing she'd be asleep by now, it'd upset Lil even more if she had to look into Anne's bottle-green eyes, alight with anticipation, and tell her she'd not been Cinderella after all, she'd gone to the ball, but she'd not sung with her Prince Charming, she'd run off and left him playing the piano to a pub full of revellers who'd turned up to see Lillian Cooper and might well be clamouring for their money back.

But what if Dorrie had let Anne stay up a bit? Seeing as how it was a special night? Tessa glanced up at the lamplight flickering in the first floor window as she helped an increasingly more unsteady Lil up the steps to the front door of the shop.

She'd leave her down here, she decided. That'd be best. She'd get her sitting down in the small kitchen and she'd run upstairs first and check the coast was clear.

Lil had started to shiver quite a bit. Be the shock more than the cold, Tessa thought, as she rummaged around in her handbag for the front door key. She needed a warm by the fire, get her feeling halfway normal again, and a cup of tea, maybe a tipple of something to steady her nerves.

'Tess.'

She'd just got the key in the lock when she heard his voice. A voice she could have picked out among thousands, yet for a second she didn't believe it was him. He'd not written and told her to expect him, had he?

But she'd sat out here, on this step, and wished for him.

Slowly, she turned round, her heart leaping about in her chest like a rabbit's foot.

He was there. Standing at the foot of the steps, his kitbag slung over his shoulder, looking strangely unnatural out of his uniform, his hazel eyes fixed on her.

'Matthew!'

She'd have flown straight back down the steps and pulled him into her arms, it was all she wanted to do, but she still had the weight of Lil leaning heavily against her. If she moved so much as a muscle the pair of them would go tumbling down on to the pavement.

She needed to get Lil inside, to deliver her safely into a chair. She needed both arms free so she could hold Matthew tight.

'Wait, let me just . . . ' With difficulty she held Lil up with one arm, grappling about in the darkness with the other hand to open the shop door.

It felt all wrong, to be like this, for Matthew to be in touching distance when she'd waited and worried for so long, and yet she was having to keep him waiting while she sorted Lil out.

'Here, give her to me.' Matthew appeared at Tessa's elbow, reaching an arm around Lil so she sagged against him instead. 'Get that door open, Tess.'

She got the lamp lit; pulled up a chair for Lil, but Matthew had lifted her up into his arms. He looked every bit the hero, Tessa thought, her heart twisting at the sight of him in the soft lamplight, carrying Lil as though she weighed no more than Victor did.

'What's got into you, eh?' Matthew

murmured to Lil, and she nestled into his coat.

'Matthew, you're home. Tessa, she's been waiting . . . ' She came to a bit then, suddenly realised what was going on. 'I'm all right. I can manage.'

But Matthew kept a firm hold of her.

'Tess can wait five minutes. Come on, let's get you upstairs and in the warm.'

He carried her up, with not so much as a glance in Tessa's direction.

She couldn't make a fuss, she told herself sternly; Lil was her friend and she was that cold and knocked for six her legs weren't even working properly.

Hadn't she been determined to get her safely home? Shouldn't make a difference that Matthew was here.

But he'd said more to Lil than he'd said to Tessa, his wife. Didn't seem as though he was all that keen to look at her, either. And he'd said she could wait five minutes, as though it didn't matter, as though she'd not been waiting so long already that every second more was an absolute agony.

Why didn't he understand that?

This was all wrong. He'd be cross with her, of course he was, over the whole Iris Phelps business, and Victoria, even more so. But she loved him, and he was home safe. Why didn't that matter most?

Matthew deposited Lil into the armchair by the fire, just as Dorrie hurried out from the kitchen, wiping her hands on a tea towel.

'Lil? What's happened? Matthew! Good to see you home, love.' She turned expectantly to Tessa. 'Whatever's happened to Lil?'

'She couldn't do it,' Tessa told her flatly. 'She wasn't ready, Dorrie. She should never have gone.'

Dorrie arched an eyebrow at her.

'That's me told then, is it?' She nodded towards the kitchen. 'Kettle's not long boiled. Make us up a pot, looks like Lil could do with thawing her bones, and I reckon your Matthew's earned himself a cuppa. Go on, Tess. I'll look after Lil.'

Tessa did as she was told, she'd no energy to argue. She'd have something to say about it, though, if Dorrie started on at Lil, if she even hinted that she'd let her Bertie down, she'd tell her straight.

She found a cloth and lifted the kettle, sloshing boiling water into the pot before she'd even thought to check if Dorrie had added tea leaves to the strainer. It was empty, and she'd not noticed. She'd have to start again.

Carefully she emptied the teapot back into the kettle. It would do her good to concentrate on something, even if it was something as simple as brewing the tea. She'd not stop feeling all heavy inside, but at least it'd be easier to keep the tears hidden.

She went to reach for the tea caddy, but it was placed gently into her hand. She was aware of Matthew then, standing behind her, waiting, while she spooned tea leaves into the strainer. He reached up to put the caddy back for her, while she started over, pouring boiling water into the pot, and when she'd nothing left to do but wait for it to brew, he pulled her into his arms and held her tight.

'I missed you, Tess.'

She sagged against him, weak with relief. He was here, he was safe, and he'd missed her.

Secrets and Lies

A faint grey light was starting to seep through the window of the tiny top floor kitchen as Tessa struck a match and lit the gas under the kettle. Most days she was up at this hour, creeping about as quiet as a mouse so she'd not wake Anne and Victor.

Weekdays in particular called for a quick cup of tea followed by a brisk pace along Hockley Street if she was to be ensconced behind her machine in good time for the start of her shift at the factory.

She was at liberty to dally a little more on a Saturday, but with it being the only full day she was free to work in the shop, she'd make a cup of tea, grab an apple for breakfast and pad downstairs in her stockings to get cracking on customer orders a good hour or two before it was time to turn the sign.

It didn't matter what day it was today. Matthew's first day back home she'd be spending with him, and if folk took offence she'd worry about it tomorrow. It was a Saturday, as it happened, so at least she'd not end up getting her marching orders from old Ambrose.

But she'd been up with the lark all the same. She'd waited so long to have Matthew back with her — he was here now and she was determined not to waste a minute. It felt a bit like Christmas, she mused, as she laid out the tea tray. That feeling of delicious anticipation she'd got when she was a starry-eyed little girl, delving into her stocking to discover the small gifts for which Hilary had somehow managed to scrape together a few bob.

She felt it again now, waiting for Matthew to finish shaving.

They'd take the tram out of Birmingham, she decided. Walk up to the Lickey Hills, just like they used to. She'd make a picnic basket so they could stay there all day, strolling hand in hand through the woods until they found a spot where they could settle for a bit, and there'd just be them, and the sun and the trees, and it'd be perfect.

With the tea brewing under the cosy, Tessa carried the tray into the lounge. It was cosy in there, with a gentle glow from the oil lamp. She'd make the tea and pour them a cup, and hopefully they'd have time yet before Bea put in an appearance.

She caught her breath in surprise when she realised Matthew was sitting quietly in the armchair. She'd not heard him walk back through from the bathroom, but then he'd have the decency not to be stomping about at this hour of the morning, same as she did.

'You gave me a start.' She smiled at him as she set the tray down on the table. 'I didn't hear you.'

Matthew averted his gaze from the flickering flames in the hearth to focus on Tessa instead. He looked blank, almost expressionless, she thought worriedly, but he'd not slept well, even back in his own bed he'd been tossing and turning.

'I'm off out in a bit,' he told her, and

she knew he'd not heard a word she'd said. He'd be teasing her if he had, chiding her for jumping out of her skin at her own shadow. He'd not heard her. He'd not even been listening.

She stole a quick glance at the clock on the mantel, as if she expected it to tell her different to what she knew, that as yet it was the wrong side of seven in the morning; where could he possibly need to be at this hour?

'Where you off to?' she asked, doing her best to keep her voice as casual as she could. Not once had she ever had to bite her tongue with Matthew, but he'd not fought a war for six years just to come home to a nagging wife.

'Thought I'd go down the depot,' he said. 'See about getting my old job back.'

'There's no hurry.' The tea nicely mashed, Tessa replaced the lid and poured them each a cup. 'Be locked up still at this hour, won't it? Petrol rationing's stopped the early bus runs.'

'Done away with half the drivers as well, I suppose.' Matthew expelled a ragged sigh. 'Not got a chance, have I?'

'It's worth a try, if that's what you want.' Tessa handed him his tea. 'Drink that first, though. It's brass monkey weather out there.'

'Thanks.' Matthew ran a finger absent-mindedly around the rim of his cup. 'I can't just sit around, I need a job.'

'But you're tired,' she persisted. 'Matthew, you hardly slept a wink. If there's a job going at the depot it'll still be there tomorrow.'

'Of course it won't.' He shook his head, looking at her like he thought her a bit slow. 'Tess, there's more men coming back every day than there's jobs to go round them all. Reckon I'm already too late.'

'Even if you are, even if there's nothing going, it won't leave us destitute,' Tessa reasoned. 'I'm on a decent wage at the factory and the shop's bringing in a fair bit.'

'So I've no need to earn a penny, is that it?' Matthew asked bitterly. 'You expect me to just sit here and twiddle my thumbs while yon work all the hours to keep us both? I won't do that, Tess. I don't care if you're spinning rags into gold in that shop of yours.'

He wasn't the sort to sit back and watch life pass him by, but why did he have to rush off down the depot when they'd had all of five minutes together? She'd got up this morning intending to leave the shop closed because all she wanted was to spend this day, all of it, with Matthew, talking to no-one but him, holding his hand tight, having a few hours of just them before they got on with picking up the pieces.

But he'd got up this morning wanting only to get his old job back, he'd been thinking about that instead of about her, as if it was more important.

Hundreds of times he'd flown headfirst into enemy fire, but they'd not got him. Night after night she'd huddled in the Anderson, ears strained to hear the whistle and crunch of bombs dropping outside, and each time she'd emerged with her life intact.

It was hard to see how the rest of it mattered. If they lived on a crust of bread between them from now on, at least they'd be living.

'I thought we could go up to the Lickeys,' she suggested. 'Have a day out, just you and me.'

Matthew looked away from her.

'I've things to do, Tess.'

'It won't take you all day to get to the depot and back.'

'Not just that. Other things.' He looked back at her accusingly, as if it was all her fault.

Perhaps it was. He had Victoria to fetch home, didn't he? Only right he should put her welfare above a selfish day out in the country. The sooner she was back home where she belonged, the sooner she'd start to settle.

Then there was the matter of Iris. Tessa hadn't asked him about Iris yet, who she was, why she'd shown up in Hockley Street in the middle of the night. There'd be plenty of time for all that, she'd thought. For now she and

Matthew mattered, and the rest of the world would have to wait.

But it was Tessa who'd ended up waiting, Matthew had his old job to see about, his niece to fetch, he'd perhaps be dropping in on Iris Phelps, too, seeing as Tessa had made such a mess of things there.

He'd no time to wander hand in hand with his wife through a forest of trees as if tomorrow would do for the rest of it. He didn't even want to. Tessa felt sad to her bones as she watched him deposit his still half-full cup down on to the table and get determinedly to his feet.

'I'd best be off then,' he told her. 'Won't find a job sat here, will I?' He glanced down at her briefly, before he turned to go. 'You've the shop to open anyway, Tess. We can't just flit off when the fancy takes us.'

Life had to go on, she conceded, as she sat and listened to the faint tread of his footsteps descending the stairs. She knew there was every sense in him going to ask after his old job as soon as he felt up to it, but she'd wanted this day with him, she'd looked forward to it.

Why didn't he want that, too? Why had he gone out already, when it'd be a good hour or more yet before the depot was unlocked? The thought of having to talk to her and he was off traipsing the streets before the sun had risen.

No, she'd not go down that road. Tessa gave herself a little shake, downing the rest of her tea in one go and scalding her throat a bit, but at least it stopped her giving way to tears. All those women who'd lost their husbands for ever, they'd every right to self-pity, but she'd got Matthew back, safe and in one piece. She'd take him in this frame of mind over not having him at all any day of the week.

'Where's Matthew took himself off to at this unearthly hour?' Bea enquired, buttoning her housecoat to the neck to ward off the dawn chill as she shuffled into the kitchen. 'And is there any tea on the go?'

'Fresh in the pot as of five minutes ago.' Tessa ran water into the sink, chasing the dregs of Matthew's tea down the plughole. 'He's gone to see about getting his old job back.'

'Post-war economy,' Bea grumbled. 'He'll be lucky. Are you opening the shop today?'

'Course I am. Saturday morning, Bea — think of all those women with a week's pay burning a hole in their pocket.'

Tessa kept her tone light as she washed up her and Matthew's cups.

There was no point mentioning how disappointed she was that she'd be standing behind the shop counter all day instead of walking in the countryside with Matthew. He'd no time for such frivolities, and if she cared about business at Li'l Tessa's, neither did she.

'I know it needs to be open,' Bea agreed. 'But it's Matthew's first day back, Tess. I just thought you might want to spend it with him. Ma and I can manage the shop between us.'

'Ta, Bea, I appreciate the offer, but there's no need.' Tessa forced a smile as she turned from the sink to face her friend. 'He's got things to do, so I might as well put some hours in. You and Dorrie do more than enough in the week.'

'While you're slaving away at the factory,' Bea pointed out. 'Not exactly putting your feet up, is it?' Perplexed, she narrowed her eyes at her.

'Did he say he'd be out all day then?'

'More or less.' Tessa wiped her hands on a tea towel. 'I'd best get downstairs, or I'll have a dozen customers banging the door down.'

'Stop changing the subject, Tessa. Don't wash with me, that don't. I've known you too long.' Bea plonked herself down on to a kitchen chair. 'Pull up a pew. You've a few minutes yet before you risk an angry mob on the doorstep.'

One foot already in the hallway and making a bid for freedom, Tessa hovered uncertainly. She should have guessed Bea would know her too well to miss how despondent she felt, but they weren't young girls any more, sharing whispered confidences over a cup of tea and a biscuit; the only one she wanted to talk to was Matthew. It felt disloyal to him to be discussing this with anyone else, even her good friend, Bea.

'I need to be making a start on those orders,' she protested.

'They'll get done the same if you start them now or in five minutes,' Bea said bluntly. 'Tess, I don't mean to pry, but if you and Matthew have had words, the shop's the last thing you should be fretting about.'

Tessa glanced at her sharply.

'We've not rowed. He's just busy, and so am I.'

Bea arched an eyebrow incredulously.

'This the same Matthew that's been pining for you non-stop for the past six years, is it? When we first joined up, me and him, you were all he went on about, Tess. We'd go out to dances in town and he'd sit and talk about you all night.' She smiled, remembering. 'He loves the bones of you, and I know how much he's missed you. What's so important you can't put it aside, just for one day?'

'I'd thought about leaving the shop

closed,' Tessa admitted. 'I wanted us to go up to the Lickeys for the day, but Matthew's got things to do.'

'So wait for him to get back and whisk him off then.'

As if it were as easy as that, Tessa thought.

'He won't want to,' she said flatly.

'Of course he will. He loves you.' Bea rummaged around the biscuit tin for a custard cream. 'I'll hold the fort, I promise. Or don't you trust me with your little empire?'

'You know I do.' Tessa smiled at her. 'Don't be daft.'

'Ditto. Whatever's gone wrong, put it right. You've been waiting for ever to have him back with you, Tess.' Bea rammed the lid back on to the biscuit tin, just as Victor's demanding wail burst up through the floorboards.

'Action stations then. If Victor's up and bawling for his breakfast, reckon it's high time I was dressed and earning my keep.' She aimed a smile at Tessa. 'I'm grateful that you agreed to me working in the shop.'

'Why wouldn't I?'

'It's yours and Lil's, isn't it? Got it up and running nicely between the two of you, then I waltz back and start shoving my nose in.'

Might not be up and running for much longer, Tessa mused, as she hurried down the stairs. Here was Bea thinking she'd landed on her feet working in the shop, and if Lil decided to sell up, she'd find herself out on her ear and scrabbling around for a job, same as Matthew was.

Or perhaps Bea already knew of Lil and Bertie's plans. Being family, proper family, perhaps she'd been told. That would explain why she saw nothing wrong in packing Tessa off for a day in the country with Matthew.

Bea knew it didn't matter either way. Li'l Tessa's would be boarded up soon enough.

Matthew was the one she wanted to confide in about it, Tessa thought, as she unlocked the shop. He was her best friend, the one she trusted above all others. To keep to herself something that worried her this much felt all wrong and unnatural, but she couldn't worry him with it, especially if he came back later to say he'd had no luck getting his old job back.

Time was he'd never have let her get away with keeping anything from him, he'd have seen it in her eyes as soon as he looked at her, but he was distracted, and keeping enough secrets of his own, she thought, her heart twisting as she imagined him pacing the streets in the early morning chill. Last night she'd asked him why she'd not had a letter telling her he was coming home. Not that it mattered, not really, but she'd have been there to meet him off the train. She'd have been there to hold him tight the second he stepped back on to Birmingham soil.

'Thought I'd surprise you,' he'd said, and he'd frowned at her. 'Thought you'd be happy to see me, Tess.'

Happy didn't cut it. She was over the moon. But after the mystery of Iris Phelps, and his refusal to discuss in his letters what they'd do about fetching Victoria, and now he'd sloped off down the bus depot a good hour or more before he'd a hope of being seen, the fact she'd not had a letter telling her to expect him was just one more secret he'd kept from her.

'Right, it's all sorted,' Bea announced, striding into the shop moments later. 'Ma and me, we're going to look after the shop, and Victor, between us. Bertie's taking Lil out for the day, and you, Auntie Tess, are chaperoning my niece into town to spend her pocket money.'

Tessa glanced up from the shop counter, where she was pinning the hem of a skirt, half-a-dozen pins gripped between her teeth. Discarding them into her cupped palm so she could speak, she nodded towards the boxes of material stacked up in the corner.

'This here skirt's the first of a long list of orders, Bea. Not that I don't enjoy every minute of our Anne's company, but I can't swan off and leave you with this lot.'

'Don't see why not.' Decision made as far as she was concerned, Bea took up residence behind the counter, opening a drawer to retrieve Tessa's order book. 'I know my way around a sewing-machine same as you. The designs are the hard part, and you've got them done and dusted already. All us amateurs have to do is stitch it all together.'

'You're hardly an amateur, Bea.'

'So I know what I'm doing, then.' Bea knotted a headscarf around her auburn curls. 'Have a day off for once, Tess. Take our Anne to a cafe and treat the pair of you to an enormous cake. Be better for you than moping over Matthew all day,' she added, eyebrows arched pointedly as she smiled at Tessa. It was on the tip of her tongue to protest that she'd retire her sewing-machine for good before she allowed one imperfect stitch to find its way into a customer's basket, but it was true her heart wasn't really in it today, Tessa conceded.

Bea had changed her tune, though — it wasn't five minutes since she was all for manning the shop so that Tessa could lay in wait with a picnic basket to whisk Matthew off to the tram stop soon as he walked back through the door, and now she'd decided Tessa should whisk Anne off into town for a cream cake instead.

Still, she might as well. What else was she meant to do? Sit around and wait until Matthew sloped back through the door? If he didn't want to spend time with her, perhaps Anne would.

By the sounds of it she'd be helping Lil out, and that was the most important part.

It felt like Matthew's coming back suddenly, and Lil's anguish as she'd crept home from the Black Horse with her head on Tessa's shoulder was days ago, but it had been just hours since Lil had dashed off the stage and fled down Gerard Street as if the crowd itself had been snapping at her heels.

She'd need support this morning, Tessa reminded herself. No matter what else was going on, Lil would need her friends. She mustn't let her own sadness over Matthew blinker her to how hurt Lil was feeling.

'Bertie's talked Lil into a day out then, has she?' she asked wryly. 'Or is he just hoping for the best as usual?'

'Reckon he's learned his lesson there,' Bea said quietly. 'She's agreed to it, he said. They're driving out to Kenilworth.'

'They had their honeymoon there,' Tessa remembered. Bea nodded.

'Bertie's on about taking her round some of the places they went to. Reminder of happier times, I suppose. Help her remember why she fell for our Bertie in the first place.'

'Lil loves Bertie,' Tessa said. 'That's not changed.'

'Same as Matthew still loves you,' Bea replied bluntly. 'But life gets in the way sometimes. Think Lil feels a bit brighter today, anyway. It seems to have done her the world of good, having Ma to talk to last night.'

'It would do,' Tessa agreed. 'She's in need of a mum, it'll do her good. I'm glad Dorrie had the sense not to go on at her for leaving Bertie high and dry.'

Bea chuckled softly.

'And risk you climbing back up on your high horse, Tessa? You know Ma thinks a lot of Lil. She'll not see her fretting if she can do a bit to help.' She cast a thoughtful eye around the shop. 'She likes working in here, Ma does. You're not to worry about anything today, Tess. You take our Anne out for a look round the shops, and Ma and I will look after this place.'

'I been saving up, Auntie Tess,' Anne announced proudly, her small hand clutching Tessa's as they set off along Hockley Street. 'I got eight shillings in my purse.'

'You're the richest of all of us then.' Tessa smiled down at the little face, all bright eyes and cheeks flushed with anticipation.

It would do Anne good, this trip into town, as much good as it would do her mother to be off in the car with Bertie for a bit of peace and quiet away from Birmingham. Anne knew all right, she was far too sharp to miss how sad Mummy looked, or how the grown-ups talked in hushed voices whenever she was in hearing distance.

She'd not forget, Anne wouldn't; her brow creased in a frown whenever she watched Lil and worried about her; but she was looking forward to a trip out with Auntie Tess. It would distract her for an hour or two at least, Tessa thought, as she rummaged in her own purse for the bus fare.

It wasn't all that far to walk to town, but she'd promised Anne a bus ride as a special treat. So rarely did they use the buses, and Anne enjoyed sitting up on the top deck, kneeling on the seat with her nose pressed up against the window, watching the streets of Birmingham float by.

Anne scrambled up on to her knees, tugging her coat sleeve down over her palm and raising her fist to rub at the grimy window.

'Hold it right there, little lady.' Tessa raised an eyebrow at her, mock sternly, making Anne giggle. 'You'll get me in trouble, you will. Here, use my glove.'

Anne rubbed a circle in the grime, a small window to the world outside.

'Daddy's taking Mummy out in the car,' she said after a moment of watching the streets drift by. 'They're going to the country to see trees and animals and flowers.' She turned to look at Tessa. 'Mummy said she'd bring me back a buttercup.'

'Did she now?' Tessa smiled at her. 'Then we'd better make sure we have a vase ready.'

She wondered if Anne minded that her parents had gone without her, if she felt lonely that she'd been left behind, even if she was off to town to spend her pocket money.

'No flowers out there.' Anne pressed her nose back up against the glass. 'Them houses are broken,' she noted solemnly, as they passed a row of bombed-out shells. 'Mummy's sad that she lives here. She wants to live in a big castle in the country, like Cinderella. She told me.'

'That'd make you a real princess, wouldn't it?'

Tessa kept the smile fixed on her face. She'd not let Anne see how troubled she was by the mere suggestion that Lil might move away from Birmingham. Li'l Tessa's would well and truly be a whim of the past if that happened.

Was it just a child's fanciful thinking? Or her mother's, even? Or was Lil seriously contemplating a move out to the country? She'd grown up in a sleepy Welsh village; was she thinking of returning to the life she knew best?

It would certainly be a happier and healthier childhood for Anne and Victor, Tessa pondered sadly, her mind drifting instantly to Victoria, and the wrench it would be for her to exchange the rich, green life of the countryside for the dull, grey, sombre drudge of the city.

'We found some flowers here, remember?' she reminded Anne brightly. 'When we went on our treasure hunt in the park? You just have to know where to look.'

Anne nodded thoughtfully.

'Might spend my money on a present for Mummy,' she decided. 'She can put it in her treasure box. Are we nearly there, Auntie Tess?'

'Next stop the market square,' Tessa confirmed, holding out her hand for Anne to take. 'Ready, Miss Cooper?'

In the days when she and Bea had wandered round the Bull Ring of a Saturday afternoon, debating lipstick shades and hemlines, the Market Hall had been alive with stalls of all description, selling everything from sweets to crockery.

Then it had been bombed, leaving nothing but a shell of smoking rafters, and though the stallholders had picked themselves back up and got on with it, as Birmingham folk tended to do, it hadn't been the same since.

Still, there were a fair few stalls up and running. Toy stall for one, Tessa noted, delighting in the way Anne's face lit up when she spotted it.

She'd not whine and tug at Tessa's arm the way some children did, though, no matter how her eight shillings would be burning a hole in her pocket. Besides, she'd vowed to spend her money on a present for Lil.

'Where shall we look first?' Tessa asked her.

'Want to buy something for Mummy,' she pondered. 'She'd like something pretty.'

'How about we visit the jewellery stall then? Bet we can find something pretty to go in Mummy's treasure box.'

They'd not even reached the jewellery stall when Anne stopped abruptly in front of a sparsely laden table. Amongst the few odds and ends that made up the old stall was an emerald brooch, faded a little with age and in need of a bit of a polish, Tessa noted when she picked it up to inspect it more closely, but it still glistened in the palm of her hand.

'Same colour as your eyes,' she told Anne.

'Call it a shilling and you've a bargain, m'duck,' the stallholder, a wizened old man, declared cheerily. 'Worth a king's ransom in its day, was that there brooch.

Pinned to the bodice of Queen Victoria herself, it was.'

Tessa raised both eyebrows at him.

'Come off it, Joe. Keep your tall tales for them who've not heard it all before. We'll give you sixpence for it.'

'There's no pulling the wool with you, Tess.' Joe chuckled as he took the shilling Anne handed over, duly placing sixpence change into her outstretched palm. 'There you go, little miss. For you, is it?'

'For my mummy,' Anne corrected him proudly.

'And won't it look smashing on her?' Joe glanced back at Tessa. 'My Mary's missed you browsing her haberdashery stall of a Saturday afternoon, Tess. Busy in the shop, are you?'

'Run off our feet,' Tessa told him. 'I'll pop and see her while we're here.'

'Aye, lass, she'd like that.'

They'd been working the market for donkey's years, Joe and Mary had. Him with his odds and ends, treasures of all description that needed little more than a

194

dust and a polish, and her with her array of buttons, ribbons, braid and lengths of material all the colours of the rainbow.

It was nice to see, Tessa thought, the pair of them just a few yards away from each other, day after day.

She could imagine Lil and Bertie like that. Years from now, when they were old and grey, they'd still be devoted to each other.

Saturday afternoon in a matter of hours now, and for the first time in months Bertie wouldn't be at his piano, playing his regular set to the customers at the Black Horse. Bertie was driving his Lil out to the country, for a day of just enjoying each other's company.

Tessa swallowed the sudden lump in her throat. It wasn't fair to Anne to give way to tears now, and she'd be causing a bit of a spectacle of herself anyway, blubbing in the middle of the market square.

'Right, then,' she said brightly. 'Toy stall next?'

Anne found what she was looking for straightaway. She'd not known exactly what that was, not until she spotted him, but then she had eyes for nothing else.

'Have I got enough money, Auntie Tess?'

'You will have.' Tessa opened her purse, just in case. The way Anne was cuddling the little brown bear, it would break her heart if she had to put him back and choose something else. 'I'll give you some money if you need a bit extra.'

'That'll be seven and six for the bear,' the young woman behind the stall informed them in a soft Welsh lilt.

He was fated to be Anne's — after buying Lil's brooch Anne had left in her purse seven and six to the penny.

So intent was Tessa on hovering protectively over Anne while she counted out her coins into the young woman's hand, only when the little bear was safely in Anne's arms, did she glance up into a face she recognised instantly.

The woman working the toy stall was Iris Phelps.

She was making an honest living for herself then, Tessa mused, as she sat in the cafe with Anne a few moments later. Better that than a life of crime, or perhaps it was only Tessa's coat she'd fancied pinching.

Soon as she recognised Tessa, she'd grabbed her money bag and slipped out the back of the stall, disappearing into such a densely packed market square that Tessa had known she'd no hope of catching her. If she'd been on her own she'd have torn after her anyway, but it wouldn't do to drag Anne along on a wild goose chase.

So Iris Phelps had got away all over again, and Tessa was consoling herself with a eup of tea and a custard slice, while across the table from her, Anne solemnly shared her hot buttered tea-cake and cherry pop with Rupert, her new bear.

'Reckon Rupert will be great pals with Rosie Rabbit,' Tessa told her. 'Be up to all sorts, the pair of them.'

Anne nodded, and her face was one big smile as she finished off the last of her teacake.

'Ta, Auntie Tess. Mummy will like her brooch as well, won't she?'

'Course she will. We'll go home and polish it so it's all sparkly for her, shall we?'

There was just one more stop Tessa wanted to make before she and Anne caught the bus back to Hockley Street. Not back to the toy stall; Iris would be like a rabbit in headlights now, all on edge expecting Tessa to march back over to her and demand her coat back. Well, she'd not put Anne through that. She'd come back later.

It was the bus depot Tessa headed for, Anne's hand clutched tightly in hers. It wouldn't hurt to pop in, to see if Matthew had got his old job back, and to add her own two pence worth if he hadn't. Do her good, having Anne there; she'd not be able to rant and rave, she'd have to keep it civil.

Alf Piatt, who ran things at the depot, was only too pleased to see her.

'Mrs Lane! Been a few years, ain't it?'

'Six at last count, Mr Piatt,' Tessa

replied politely. 'Surprised you remember me.'

'Never forget a face, I don't,' Alf declared solemnly. 'When's your Matthew back from that war then? Or are you down here wanting a job for yourself?'

Taken aback, Tessa blinked at him.

'He got back last night. Has he not been to see you?'

Alf shook his head resolutely.

'Not a sign of him, Mrs Lane. Expecting him down here, were you?'

'He'll have got held up,' she lied. 'He had a fair bit to see to, with it being his first day back. He'll be along later.'

'Aye, well, when he does show up I'll have him back driving them buses, don't you fret on that,' Alf promised her. 'Awash with folk who can drive a bus I might be, but I'm telling you, Mrs Lane, there's not many who know the streets of Brum like your Matthew. There'll always be a job here for him if he wants it.'

Tessa walked slowly back to the bus stop, Anne and Rupert Bear skipping alongside. So Matthew had his old job back, though as yet he didn't know it.

But why didn't he know it yet? He'd said he was going straight there this morning. Where did Matthew go instead?

She'd not fret over it, Tessa told herself firmly. He was an adult, he was free to go where he pleased; he didn't have to account for every minute of his day. Maybe he'd just wanted to walk around Birmingham for a while.

Anyway, it'd ease his mind when he did go to see Alf. Thinking this, Tessa felt a bit brighter as she sought out the right coins for their bus fares.

Knowing he had a job to go to, Matthew would perhaps feel more like spending time with her.

He'd not felt like it today, he'd had too much else to do, but for Bea, his friend and one-time comrade in the air force he'd found time to sit in the shop and talk to her as she ran hemlines under the needle of her sewing-machine.

Anne dashed straight over to show her new bear to Auntie Bea, and slowly

Matthew looked up to meet Tessa's gaze. There was a cold, hardened look in his eyes, and it made her shiver.

'Have you been to the depot?' she asked him quietly, and he nodded.

'There's nothing going, Tess.'

She felt cold to her bones. Why was he lying to her?

He'd not been anywhere near the depot this morning, that was clear, but by the time Tessa and Anne left for town, he'd already been out hours.

Where had he really gone to?

The Shop Changes Hands

It was as if the mere sight of her had pulled Matthew up sharp, Tessa thought. Before she could say a word he was up off his chair and buttoning his coat, the glance he aimed at his watch a cursory one; no matter where the hands were pointing he'd made his mind up to be off out again rather than stay one more minute under the same roof as his wife.

'Where are you going now?' she asked him quietly. She'd not make a fuss, not with Anne in earshot. 'Can you spare one minute first?'

Matthew tugged his coat collar up round his throat.

'I've a train to catch,' he said, matter-of-factly. 'I'd best get a move on.'

Panic gripped Tessa. A train to where? Was he leaving her? He'd been back with her less than twenty-four hours, but had it been enough for him to know without hesitation that he'd made a mistake coming back here?

Was that why he'd not bothered going down the depot? There was no point going after a job if he'd no intention of sticking around to do it.

'Where?' she whispered hoarsely, clearing her throat when Anne glanced up at her in alarm. She tried again. 'Where are you catching a train to, Matthew?'

'Wales,' he told her. 'Need to fetch Victoria, don't I?'

Tessa breathed out slowly. Of course he did. Hadn't she known that was on his mind first thing this morning when he'd told her he had things to do? Of course Victoria should be at the top of his list. But for a minute there sheer panic had set in, blinding her to all other possibilities but the one that frightened the life out of her.

'Take Tess with you,' Bea suggested. 'Be a nice trip out together, won't it? She's not needed here today,' she added, with the smug superiority of knowing she'd presented them with a watertight argument. 'And our Anne can keep me company, can't you, poppet?'

'I can help in the shop,' Anne decided excitedly. 'Can I, Auntie Bea?'

'I'm counting on it.' Bea smiled at her. 'You'll be the best assistant anyone ever had.'

Tessa's heart lifted a little. Why shouldn't she go with Matthew to fetch Victoria? He'd perhaps relent and talk to her a bit once they'd left Birmingham far behind them.

She glanced at Matthew; he shrugged, not quite meeting her eye, but at least he'd not refused point blank.

'What about you?' she asked Bea, nodding her head towards the crib in the corner, where Victor was sound asleep. 'Can you manage? Where's Dorrie got to?'

'Ma's just popped into town,' Bea informed her. 'She'll be back in a bit. Besides, it'll be quiet now 'til closing time. We can manage, can't we, little miss shop lady?'

Anne nodded emphatically.

'There you go.' Bea smiled. 'All in hand. Go, Tess.' She looked at her pointedly. 'Be with Matthew.'

'If you're sure,' Tessa agreed, but when she turned to Matthew, the look in his eyes broke her heart.

'Aren't you needed here, Tess? What with Lil feeling out of sorts?' His eyes ran the length of her. 'Bitter out there, it is. Where's your ma's coat?'

'Misplaced it,' she murmured flatly. Now wasn't the time to start on about Iris Phelps.

'It were swiped off its peg right in front of her nose, more like,' Bea chimed in. 'Still, that one she's wearing does the trick, don't it, Tess? Not quite up to shop standard but if she gets the shivers on the way to Wales, she's got you to hold her tight and keep her warm, Matthew.'

Tessa aimed a sharp glare at Bea, willing her to be quiet. She didn't want Matthew railroaded into taking her with him, she wanted him to want her by his side, and she knew he didn't. He wanted to go alone.

He perhaps thought she'd go upsetting Victoria all over again. With Hilary gone, Matthew was the closest relative Victoria had, the only one left who had a proper duty to do what was best for her. He should put her first, Tessa thought sadly. He wouldn't be Matthew if he did any less than that.

She linked her arm through his.

'Come on,' she said firmly. Turning her back on Bea's perplexed expression, she accompanied him down the steps and into the street, but she gripped his arm a minute longer before she let him walk away from her.

'Matthew, I went to the depot.'

He stared at her.

'You went behind my back?'

'I went to see if you'd had any luck, and to say my piece if you hadn't.'

'So you don't think I can ask after my own job.'

She'd not point out he hadn't, Tessa thought. Now wasn't the time for recriminations, not when he was about to walk off and leave her for hours on end. There was a better reason why she'd gone to speak to Alf Piatt at the depot, a reason that ran miles deeper.

'You want me out from under your feet, is that it?' The look in Matthew's eyes was accusing as he faced her.

Tessa gazed at him in disbelief. This morning he'd been so intent on finding a job; it had been she who'd told him to hang fire for a bit.

'You were so determined to get your job back,' she reminded him quietly. 'It seemed so important to you. That's why I went down there; because I love you.'

He swallowed, taken aback.

'Don't matter anyway. I don't need to set foot anywhere near to know I haven't a hope.'

'That's where you're wrong.' Tessa reached for his hand. 'Alf said your old job's yours if you want it. He said no-one knows the streets of Brum like you do and he'll have you back soon as you're ready.'

Matthew's hand in hers stayed as still as if it were made of stone. Not one attempt did he make to entwine his fingers with hers.

'I've got Victoria to see to first,' he mumbled, looking past her to fix his gaze on the busy street, but Tessa knew he wasn't seeing any of it. 'Can't see us making the last train back, Tess, so it'll be Monday at the earliest, all right?'

Tessa nodded, swallowing the lump in her throat.

'I expect Peg won't mind making the spare bed up, seeing as she's got no leg to stand on this time.'

'Nor did she last time,' Matthew said with a sudden ferocity as he peeled off his heavy overcoat. 'Here, Tess. You'll catch a chill in that flimsy jacket.'

'It's not that bad.' She smiled wanly. 'Not a patch on what I make for the customers, maybe.'

Matthew draped his own coat over her shoulders, pulling it tightly around her.

'There. That'll keep you warm.'

'What about you?' Tears pooled in her eyes as she gazed at him.

'You'll be the one catching a chill, going all the way to Wales and back without a coat on.'

'I'll be all right.' He pulled her close, planting a brief kiss on the top of her head. 'I'd best go, Tess. Be too late in the day, else, and there'll be no point going.'

'So wait and go on Monday.' The words were out of her mouth before she could edit them. If she could just persuade him to wait a bit, they could have tomorrow together. There were no trains on a Sunday, no bus routes he should be driving, no opening hours in the shop for her. They could have the whole day together.

But she knew he'd made his mind up; he was travelling down to Granny Peg's cottage this evening.

At least he'd talked to her a bit first, Tessa tried to console herself. He'd not run off to the station with hardly a word between them. At least he'd remembered he cared about her.

She pulled Matthew's coat tightly around her as she watched him walk off down Hockley Street, closing her eyes and breathing in the scent of him.

She knew he loved her, no matter what

passed between them, she knew that.

So why did she feel as bereft as if it were six years ago and she was losing him all over again?

She stood there for a long time, watching him grow smaller and fainter, until she could no longer see him at all.

It was nice, having Matthew's coat on. It was like having his arms wrapped around her. She buried her gloveless hands into the pockets, the fingers of her right hand automatically curling around the solitary crumpled-up note she found in there.

She wasn't in the habit of searching through Matthew's pockets; she'd never felt the need to. There was no reason why she should start now, but her fingers tightened around the note all the same.

Where had he been this morning? Why didn't he want to spend time with her? Chances are this note would be no more than a hastily discarded train ticket from his journey home yesterday, but he was being so closed off from her, did it matter if she looked?

She stared at the note lying in her hand. It wasn't a ticket of any description. Warily she unfolded it, the words she saw hastily scrawled across it in Matthew's unmistakeable, almost illegible script, all blurred at first as she struggled to place the address she knew she recognised.

In a moment it came to her. Hilary's erstwhile address, the house she'd been allocated for her and Victoria, the house they'd never set foot in because she'd given the keys to Tessa and asked her to house-sit for her so she could spend one last evening with her mother, the house Tessa had been safe and sound in while across town Hilary and Esme had lost their lives in a bomb blast.

The housing corporation had wasted no time in reclaiming the keys from Tessa. The house Hilary had never lived in would have been passed on to some other deserving case. It had never been her home.

So why had Matthew kept hold of the address, all crumpled up in his pocket?

She'd walk there and see, Tessa

decided. She'd nowhere else to be, nor anyone who needed her. It wouldn't do any harm to go and look in on Hilary's house. There'd be strangers living there now, but perhaps she could just reassure herself they were looking after it, the home Hilary had wanted so badly for herself and Victoria.

Across town a bit, it took her a while to get there. The sun was sinking lower in the sky by the time she turned into Belgrave Road. End of a busy day, folk scuttled past her down the hill like ants, all wanting to get home and have a sit down and a cup of tea. The odd bus rattled past, and a car or two, though of course the petrol rationing was still putting a stop to all but the most essential trips.

Lil and Bertie would perhaps be home by now, Tessa thought. She'd talk to Lil once she got back, see how she was feeling.

Matthew would be on the train now, headed for Wales. He'd be passing Hawarden, where he'd spent all that time instructing new recruits in the art of flying.

Least he'd be coming home this time. It wasn't a one-way ticket; this time he'd be coming back to her.

Number thirty-eight, Belgrave Road, she'd found it. Tessa stood on the pavement outside, not sure what to do now she was here. She'd thought only as far ahead as coming to see it, just to make sure it was still standing. It seemed important somehow, that it was.

But she'd no-one here she knew. She should just turn around and begin the long trudge back to Hockley Street.

She unclenched her palm to stare at the crumpled note she'd held on to all the way here. Is this where Matthew had been this morning? He'd been out a good while; he could have walked here and back.

She'd just knock, she decided. What harm would it do? If whoever answered took offence, she could always pretend she was looking for an old friend and she'd got the wrong address.

Passing through the gap between hedges where there'd once been a gate, she went quietly up the path to the front door and knocked once.

Still she had no idea what, or who, she expected to find. Hilary she'd certainly never clap eyes on again; she was gone, there was no bringing her back, no parallel world existing on the quieter, leafier side of Birmingham, where Hilary had survived and was living here, waiting for her daughter to return from Granny Peg's house.

But when the door opened, and Tessa came face to face with the tenant, it was almost as much of a shock as if it had been Hilary herself.

Standing in the doorway, a slight figure silhouetted against the soft lamplight inside, was Iris Phelps.

'You'll be after your coat then.' White-faced, Iris held the door open just a fraction, peeping round it like a frightened child expecting a thrashing, Tessa thought wryly.

Did she really imagine Tessa was the

sort to drag her by the throat out into the street and lay into her like a brawling old shrew? If she thought that, then why approach her for help in the first place?

'You needn't look so terrified.' Tessa put out a hand to stop Iris closing the door on her. 'I should like my coat back, yes, but to be honest I'm in shock to find you here. This was my late sister-in-law's house.'

Iris eyed her curiously.

'Matthew didn't tell you where to find me then?'

'In a way he did.'

Tessa shoved the note back into her pocket. This couldn't be a coincidence. He'd not kept this address all these years in memory of his sister. He knew of Iris so he must know she'd got her feet under the table in Hilary's house. He'd been to see her this morning, that's where he'd got to.

Only she'd been working the toy stall at the market, hadn't she?

'Have you seen Matthew?' she asked, and Iris visibly flinched at the sharp edge to her tone.

'No, I've not seen your husband, Mrs Lane. If that's who you're after.'

'I know he's not here.' Tessa applied a little more pressure to the front door as Iris upped her efforts to close it. 'I'm not accusing you of anything,' she added, as it occurred to her what Iris was afraid of. The thought was so ludicrous it made her chuckle. 'Gracious, no, if you think I'm round here as the woman scorned, you couldn't be further from the truth.'

Iris watched her dubiously.

'So you just want your coat back.'

This was a chance she shouldn't pass up, Tessa thought. If Matthew had been here before her, it would have been to check Iris was all right. But he'd not seen her, and now he'd gone off to fetch Victoria, so in his absence Tessa could try and put at least a part of it right. She'd failed her niece but she could try again to help Iris.

'Actually I could do with a cuppa if there's one on the go. It's a fair walk here from Hockley Street, you know. I'm parched.' She tried a smile. 'That's if you don't think me horribly rude for inviting myself into your home.'

'I more or less invited myself into yours,' Iris said flatly. She eyed Tessa thoughtfully a minute. 'All right, come in if you want. I suppose a cup of tea's the least I owe you. My little boy's having his tea in there, mind, so if you really are hankering after knocking me into next week I'd ask you to wait 'til he's asleep.'

'Blimey, Iris, what do you take me for?'

Tessa peeled off Matthew's coat, hanging it up on a hook by the door.

Next to her own, she noticed. Her ma's coat, large as life, looking as though it hadn't suffered all that much.

'I'll just get the kettle on then.' Iris showed her into a dimly lit room where her son was perched in his highchair, traces of jam dribbling down his chin as he demolished his tea. 'Make yourself comfortable.'

What had been a comfortable dining-room last time Tessa had set foot in it was now sparsely furnished. Aside from an old cupboard below the window-sill, the only furniture was an oblong table with three chairs around it, the little boy's highchair pulled up to the fourth side.

Tessa sat down on the nearest chair. She felt a despondency that she'd not expected. Being here, amidst such . . . not squalor; Iris might have had very little but if this room was anything to go by she kept every inch of it scrubbed; nor was it poverty, not when her little boy was attacking his toast and jam with the relish of a happy, rosy cheeked, well-fed child. Gloom then, she thought; solitude, a quiet, friendless place where the sun didn't quite seem to make it through the window.

She'd known Iris had fallen on hard times; she'd not needed to hear a word of explanation to know that. If she'd fallen on her feet she'd not have been lurking in the shadows of Hockley Street wanting a friendly shoulder, would she?

'Mam.' The boy stuck out a sticky hand towards Tessa.

'Mummy will be here in a minute,' she told him, but he shook his head, stubbornly thrusting his hand towards her.

'Jam done now.'

'All right, little man.' Tessa fished in her handbag for a handkerchief and drew her chair closer to his highchair. 'Let's get you cleaned up, shall we? Gracious, you're a bit sticky!'

'Gets it everywhere but in his mouth, he does.' Iris appeared, setting down two mismatched cups of tea on to the table. 'Here, I'll wipe him. You've not come round here to wait on my son.'

'I don't mind,' Tessa assured her. 'He's a right little charmer, isn't he? Got a bit of a twinkle in your eye, haven't you?' she told the little boy.

'Takes after his pa,' Iris murmured. 'Here's your tea, Mrs Lane. There's no sugar, I've not had time to go to the shop today.'

More likely she'd had nothing in her purse to buy it with, Tessa thought. Chances are the sugar bowl had been empty for some time.

'No matter, I don't take sugar,' she lied. 'Sweet enough already, so they tell me. And call me Tessa; this Mrs Lane business makes me sound far more grown-up than I am.'

The smile Iris managed was still a little guarded, but at least she'd stopped looking at Tessa like she expected a confrontation any minute. Her little boy had helped to break the ice a bit, Tessa thought, watching the way Iris lifted him out of his highchair, tenderly settling him on to her lap.

'What do you call him?' she asked her.

'Berwin Thomas Phelps,' Iris announced proudly.

'Berwin? There's a name I've not heard before.'

'It's Welsh, it means a blessing,' Iris explained, reaching into the pocket of her pinafore for a raggedy bear which her son grasped, chuckling delightedly to himself. 'Berwin's a bit of a mouthful, though, so I call him Tommy for short. After his pa, see.'

It was the second mention she'd made

of Tommy's pa in as many minutes, Tessa noted. Where was he then, Thomas Phelps senior? Perhaps he was off doing his bit to win the war. He'd yet to show his face under this roof anyway. She and Tommy had very much been left to fend for themselves.

'Where's Tommy's pa, Iris?' she asked. 'If I'm prying you can tell me to keep my nose out.'

Iris narrowed her eyes shrewdly.

'You've got him down as a bad 'un, you think he's took off and left us to drown, me and Tommy. Well, he didn't.'

'Was he called up?' Tessa prodded, when she hesitated. 'There's plenty still waiting to be released from service, he'll not be the last by a long shot.'

'He flew for your husband's squadron,' Iris told her. 'Fresh out of training he was, and green round the gills when he first set foot on that base, but Matthew kept an eye on him.' She smiled fondly. 'He kept writing to me how Flight Lieutenant Lane was like a big brother to him. He knew how I worried, see. Knew it'd ease my mind to read he was being looked after.'

'I know how that feels,' Tessa murmured.

'He was that proud, the first time he went up in that Spitfire,' Iris continued as if she'd not heard her. 'Earned himself a medal, my Tom did; green, black and orange ribbons.'

'That's for defending his country. Matthew's got one, too.'

Iris blinked at her in disbelief, a child unable to grasp why any of it mattered.

'They sent it to me, you know, his medal. Should have saved themselves the trouble, I don't want it. What good's a medal to me?'

There was no point telling her she'd be consoled by it, Tessa thought, that eventually she'd look back and be proud of how brave he'd been. It didn't matter, any of it; medals, ribbons, the honour of defending his country, not when he'd never come home afterwards.

Iris had lapsed into silent reverie, her hand stroking Tommy's hair. The only sound in the room was their breath, in and out. Even Tommy had ceased his cheerful chattering. He seemed to know to be quiet, as he just sat and cuddled his threadbare old teddy bear.

After a moment or two, Tessa reached across to cover Iris's cold hand with hers.

'I'm so sorry for you, Iris.'

'I wish he'd been a coward.' Iris looked up at her, tears misting her eyes. 'I didn't need him to be brave, Tessa. I needed him to be here.' She swallowed hard, her voice shaking as she continued. 'What'll I tell my Tommy when he asks where his pa is? There's just me now, me and my little boy.'

'Have you any other family?' Tessa asked her gently.

'My parents are in Birmingham,' Iris said flatly. 'That's why I came here, after Tom died. I had what was left of his pay, and not a penny more. I thought they'd help.'

'And did they?' Silly question, Tessa chided herself. Of course they hadn't, that's why Iris had turned to her instead, and she'd let her down.

'They never approved of Tom,' Iris explained. 'He came from a poorer family, see. They didn't even come to our wedding. But I thought, now Tommy's here, surely they'd want to see their grandson.'

'You'd think they would,' Tessa murmured, unable to stop herself.

'Not as if I was after free food and lodgings,' Iris said shakily. 'All I wanted was a roof over our heads until the Corporation found me a house. I'd every intention of taking whatever work I could find to support me and Tommy in the meantime. I'd not have taken a penny off them.'

'So where'd you end up instead?' Tessa asked. 'I can't imagine the Corporation were all that quick to find you this place.' She gazed around at the meagre surroundings Iris and Tommy were forced to call home, but then at least they'd a roof over their heads, she thought. More than some folk had.

'First night in Birmingham I went

down the rest centre on Moseley Road,' Iris recalled. 'Talked to an old woman there, Mrs Bryce they call her.'

Tessa nodded.

'Old Brycie, she's head of the local Women's Voluntary Service. Bit po-faced but she's got a heart of gold, she'd have helped you.'

'She knew of a room going, over the butcher's, it was.' Iris wrinkled her nose, remembering. 'With all the fragrances you'd expect from living so close to a shop full of carcasses. Still, we'd a place to lay our heads at least.' She cuddled little Tommy tighter, making him wriggle impatiently. 'Most nights I had the window open and Tommy wrapped up tight so he'd not catch a cold.'

'What about you?' Tessa asked her pointedly.

'Better chilly than smelling that all night long.' Iris sighed, and she glanced worriedly at Tessa. 'I don't want you thinking I'm ungrateful. If Mrs Bryce hadn't helped us, I don't know where we'd have ended up.'

Tessa breathed out slowly.

'You came to me for help, and I was no use to you. I'm sorry.'

'Didn't give you a chance, did I?' Iris exclaimed. 'I'd already got the room over the butcher's anyway; I weren't after a roof so much as a friendly face.' She tried a tentative smile. 'I'm the one who should be sorry. Taking off like that, and pinching your coat into the bargain. I'm not a thief, Tessa, honest I'm not. But my Tommy were having to sleep in a room that needed the window open, and your coat looked so big and warm, I just thought . . . ' she trailed off. 'If I say I weren't in my right mind it'll sound like a cop out, but it's true all the same. All I could think about were my Tommy.'

'You were being a mother,' Tessa said quietly, watching the way little Tommy snuggled into her shoulder. 'So, where's Tommy go while you're working at the market?'

'Butcher's wife watches him,' Iris said. 'Nice woman; got about twenty grandchildren so she knows how to look after babbies.'

'You could bring him to me on Saturdays,' Tessa suggested. 'Weekdays I work at Ambrose's, but on a Saturday I'm just in the shop, I could watch him.'

Was it just the guilt talking? Could she really take responsibility for young Tommy Phelps one day a week? Why not? Victor's pram was a common enough sight behind the counter; if she could keep an eye on him and serve the customers, there was no reason why she couldn't have Tommy around as well. He'd a few months on Victor so he'd not sleep as much, but he seemed a contented enough child. Besides, the shop would be a distant memory soon enough, then she'd have plenty of time on her hands to take care of him, wouldn't she?

'You've no need to do that,' Iris protested. 'You don't owe me a thing, Tessa. I'm the one should be making amends for pinching your coat.'

'Borrowed it,' Tessa corrected her. 'Not pinched. You know, if you're in need of extra blankets and the like, I've got a bit of a way with a sewing-machine. I could run you up a couple of bits and pieces?'

'It's kind of you, but I couldn't afford . . . '

'No charge,' Tessa added quickly. 'Call it a present.'

Iris's expression hardened.

'I'll not take charity,' she said stiffly.

'Don't be daft.' But she'd not push it, Tessa decided. By the sounds of it Iris worked hard for every penny she spent on food and comfort for her son, and she'd every right to be proud of that. 'A loan then,' she concluded. 'You can pay me when you're back on your feet a bit more.'

Iris nodded.

'Thank you,' she murmured. 'Tommy sleeps through now, but I do worry how he'll be when winter gets a grip.'

'I'll sort you out a couple of thick blankets,' Tessa promised her. 'One for Tommy, and one for you.'

Iris blinked at her in surprise. Of course, she'd not be expecting someone to think of her comfort, would she? Tommy's, yes, but not his mother's. Probably why she took off that night before Tessa had even got the pot brewed. She'd not believe a stranger would want to help her after she'd been turned away from her own parents' doorstep.

'Is it worth trying again to talk to your parents?' Tessa asked her gently.

'I've been past their house every day,' Iris confided. 'They've got a lamp in the front window, gives out the softest light, like a flickering fire. Shows through the curtains now the blackout's over, and it looks all homely and welcoming.'

'I think you owe it to yourself to knock on their door just once more,' Tessa ventured. 'Give them another chance to do right by you and Tommy.'

Slowly, Iris nodded.

'Maybe it's time I did.' The apprehension was back in her eyes as she looked at Tessa. 'I couldn't do it that first night, I just couldn't. Even though Tommy was fast asleep in my arms and we'd not a stitch to our name, all I kept thinking was how my parents had disapproved of Tom, and how disloyal it felt to be knocking on their door five minutes after I'd lost him.'

Tessa gazed at her, bewildered.

'So you've not even seen them?'

'I got no further than the doorstep,' Iris whispered. 'I couldn't go through with it.'

That had a familiar ring to it, Tessa thought wryly. Lil had got as far as the stage at the Black Horse; Iris had got as far as her parents' doorstep.

Neither of them had been ready to go any further, but they would be, given time. Lil would be feeling better after her run out to the country with Bertie, she'd find it in her to sing again one day. Maybe Iris just needed to work up to talking to her parents.

'You think I've no right to moan,' Iris began, but Tessa placed a hand over hers to stop her.

'I think you need your mum,' she said simply.

With her mother's coat over her arm, Tessa walked briskly back to Hockley Street. Lil would be home by now but as much as Tessa fretted over her friend, it was Matthew who took up most of her thoughts.

She was sure now that he'd wanted her to find Iris's address in his coat pocket. She'd only had to talk to Iris to know the sense of duty Matthew would be feeling towards her, the guilt he'd be struggling with because Tom Phelps, someone he'd taken under his wing, had lost his life while Matthew had returned home in one piece.

He'd never mentioned Tom in his letters; least she couldn't recall any mention of a Tom Phelps. He'd certainly not told her he'd lost a friend. She'd have remembered that. But then he'd not been allowed to write about loss of British life, in case his letter fell into the wrong hands.

Was Matthew so deeply traumatised by Tom's death that he struggled to talk of anything else? Had he needed Tessa to find out about Tom so she could talk him through it?

Tears pricked Tessa's eyelids as she pulled Matthew's coat around her. She needed him to be here, not miles away in a village in the middle of Wales.

She had her Matthew back, but she felt empty, as if they were little more than polite strangers.

It was dark by the time she got back to Hockley Street. Hours past closing time, but there was a light on still, and by the looks of it when she drew closer and could make out the silhouettes behind the blinds, no room to move in the shop, so packed with bodies it seemed to be.

A little alarmed, Tessa dashed up the steps to the front door, ferreting in her handbag for the key, but the door was opened before she could unlock it, and she was half dragged inside by an exuberant Bea Cooper.

They were all there, Dorrie, Bertie, Lil, even young Anne had obviously been allowed to stop up a bit. The shop was full of Coopers, all with glasses in their hands.

'Took your time, didn't you?' Bertie grinned at her. 'Ma's that keen to make a speech she's near enough bursting with it.'

'What's going on?' Tessa looked to Lil for an explanation, but Lil averted her eyes quicker than a rabbit down a hole, and Bea got there first.

'Bertie and Lil want to sell up, Tess, and none of us want to see this place going to strangers, so Ma's been having meetings down the bank and it's all been sorted today.' Her eyes shone as she clasped Tessa's hand. 'Ma and me, we're going into business with you.'

Tessa felt a hand on her shoulder and she turned to see Dorrie smiling apologetically at her.

'I'm sorry I've not said anything until now, Tess. I were waiting 'til I'd got the nod from the bank manager.'

'You're buying the shop?' Tessa murmured, bewildered.

'Shop, house, I'm buying every last brick!' Dorrie raised her glass to clink with Bea's. 'A toast, everyone — to my daughter and I setting up in business together! To a new era for Li'l Tessa's!'

An Uncertain Future

'We'd best make a start on these cupboards, hadn't we?' Lil tied an apron around her waist, looking every inch the sergeant major as she stood in the tiny kitchen that adjoined the shop and cast a critical eye over the worktop. She rolled up her sleeves determinedly. 'Sooner we start, sooner we'll finish.'

She'd been up since the crack of dawn, Lil had. Scarf wrapped round her curlers and still in her housecoat, she'd had her own kitchen upstairs scrubbed until it shone like a new penny and a pan of eggs bobbing away on the stove when Tessa had crept down to see who was up and about at this hour on a Sunday morning.

A world away from the shaken and subdued Lillian Cooper who'd wobbled home from the Black Horse just two nights before, this Lil had a new lease of life, a renewed sense of purpose that had her out of bed and wielding a scrubbing brush when even Victor had yet to start bawling for his breakfast.

It was as if now she'd made her mind up, she couldn't wait to get away.

There was no sense of excitement tinged with sadness, not even a remote suggestion that she might miss folk, Dorrie, Bea, Tessa; Lil had time for none of it, so intent was she on packing up her life into boxes.

They'd been planning this a while, Tessa realised. Dorrie's secret trips out to talk to the bank manager — this is what it had all been in aid of. A day or two ago, when Bertie had first mentioned to Tessa that he and Lil might sell up and move, he'd spoken as if they'd only just started to think about it, but it was crystal clear they'd been thinking about it for weeks.

Course, they'd not felt the need to consult Tessa, but then why should they? It was a family matter, and she'd not put a penny into the shop, had she? If Lil wanted to sell it, she'd be recouping her own money. Well, her Aunty Mai's money. She'd be getting it back, she'd confided to Tessa when she'd finally managed to look her in the eye after Dorrie's big announcement, every penny of it and more besides.

That's all it was to Lil, that's all it had ever been, a means of providing for her family, a sound investment opportunity once she'd caught on to how imaginative Tessa was with a needle and thread. It had made a bit of sense nonetheless, given that Lil herself knew her way around a sewing-machine, but in truth would it have really mattered if they'd dug out an allotment on one of the many bombed-out patches of wasteland and sold cabbages for a living?

To Tessa it would have mattered, but then Li'l Tessa's was her dream, and maybe she'd not put a penny into it initially, but when it came down to hours of sheer hard work, she'd put in plenty ever since.

Every Saturday standing behind that counter from dawn 'til dusk, on her feet all day when she was already tired from a week at the factory. Night after night sewing into the small hours when she had to get up for work the next morning, her eyes scratchy and sore from struggling to focus with just a faint lamplight to see by.

She'd not minded a minute of it. This was her calling, what she'd always wanted to do.

'Here, look at this, Tess. I'd forgotten we had this.' Lil lifted an old brown teapot from the depths of a cupboard. 'Do you remember?'

In the middle of sorting out cups into hers and Lil's, Tessa stopped a minute, managing a smile at the memory. 'Our lucky pot, that was. First sale we made, and we'd not even got the till installed yet, so we dropped the money in there because if we were robbed, no thief worth his salt would think to look in a teapot, but then Bertie got home and brewed us up a pot to toast our first proper sale . . .'

'. . . and we were tasting metal in our tea for weeks after,' Lil finished, a smile slowly spreading across her face. 'Poor lamb, he tries to be supportive and he ends up near enough poisoning us!'

'He'll be behind you no matter what you do.' Tessa returned her attention to the cups. 'You know he's worked for the same boss at the gas board ever since he left school? Not to mention his Saturday afternoons playing the piano down the Black Horse. There'll be a good many folk grumbling once he's packed up his songbook for the last time. Be a spotlight Jeannie has trouble filling, that will.'

She'd not meant to upset Lil; that was the last thing she wanted. If anything, she'd intended to point out just how devoted Bertie was to Lil, that he'd drop his whole life as he knew it, just because he knew it'd be the best thing for her. She'd wanted to reassure her that everything would be all right from now on, because she had Bertie by her side no matter what, and he loved her so much he was prepared to move to a new place and start his life again from scratch.

But she'd managed to offend Lil

nonetheless.

'He wants to move, same as I do,' Lil told her sharply. 'Not as if I'm dragging him there kicking and screaming, Tess. We decided this together.'

'I know that.' Tessa nodded, one hand dusting the inside of cups they'd not used for years as she continued. 'I'm sorry, Lil. I know it's the best thing for you, and that's what I was trying to say, that you've a treasure in Bertie because he'll always do what's best for you, no matter if he has to follow you to the ends of the earth to get it.'

'Wales isn't all that far,' Lil countered lightly. 'We'll just be a train ride away, and goodness knows it's a trip you've made often enough. You even know your way around my kitchen already so you'll have no trouble making a cup of tea when you visit.' She tried a smile. 'Gran will be chuffed to bits, having her great-grandchildren living under her roof. It might stop her missing Victoria so much.'

'Assuming Matthew manages to get her packed up and on the train,' Tessa commented flatly.

'Won't make no difference. She can throw all the paddies she wants, but he's her legal guardian, isn't he?' With gusto Lil wielded a cloth over the newly cleared worktop. 'He'll have her back here Monday morning, Tess.'

Back to what? What would Victoria be coming home to now? Be a right palaver under this roof, it would, what with Lil and Bertie boxing up their worldly belongings, and Dorrie going about the place with a tape measure, putting her own stamp on everything.

She'd not throw them out, Dorrie had assured Tessa. She, Matthew and Victoria, they had a home here for as long as they wanted it. The only difference would be Dorrie's name on the deeds instead of Lil's and Bertie's.

But why should she and Bea squash up on one floor when they could evict Tessa, reclaim the top floor and have a whole house to stretch out in?

There'd been times over the years when she'd felt a bit in the way, Tessa recalled, but here she'd been on hand for the shop, especially important when they'd had big orders to meet, and at a moment's notice she'd been here to lend a hand with the children.

What would they need her for now? Anne and Victor would be miles away, fussed over by Great-granny Peg, and as far as the shop was concerned, between the pair of them Dorrie and Bea would have it covered, no matter how often they pretended to be in dire need of Tessa's input.

It was turning out just as she'd feared, Tessa thought. Her home being sold from under her, because that's how it felt, and a question mark over her role as the creative mind responsible for every garment that graced the shelves.

She'd worked so hard to establish a secure future for Matthew and Victoria, and now they'd be coming home to find she was on the verge of losing it all.

Least she'd still have her job at the factory. As long as old Mr Ambrose kept the orders coming in, she'd not be destitute just yet. Demand for the serge tunics the servicemen and women wore had eased up a bit with the war coming to an end, but come Monday morning word on the factory floor was that they'd soon be reverting back to their pre-war production of cotton slips, frocks and blouses.

Her mind on Matthew, the hope she had that he'd be back from Wales with Victoria in tow by the time her shift ended tonight, Tessa let the gossip and speculation drift over her. What did it matter? If they were put to knitting socks for a living she'd not grumble. She was just grateful she had a means of paying the rent, be it for her rooms at Hockley Street, or somewhere else entirely.

Iris Phelps she'd thought of a fair bit, too, since she'd sat in her dimly lit, sparsely furnished dining-room, and heard the full extent of how she'd suffered. How secure she'd felt in comparison, Tessa thought wryly. Not that her own struggles were a patch on those Iris had faced; if she'd lost Matthew the way Iris had lost Tom, everything else would just stop mattering, and she'd not care if she never again had a roof to sleep under; but she'd sat there and offered help to Iris, not knowing her own world was just minutes away from being turned upside-down.

But she had Matthew, even if he barely had two words to utter to her, by tonight at least she'd have him home and safe. She knew about Tom Phelps now, so if that was the cause of his distress, she'd be able to talk to him about it.

At six on the dot, Tessa was first out of the gates. There'd be no stopping off at Vince Watkins's shop nor anywhere else tonight; she wanted only to dash home as quick as she could, keeping her fingers crossed that Matthew had come back, that he'd not used Victoria's reluctance to leave Granny Peg as a cast-iron excuse to stay away for a bit longer, to steer clear of his wife because he had nothing to say to her.

Buttoning up her mother's coat as she went, her hands froze suddenly, and she stopped short, near enough causing a pile-up as a long line of tired women muttered and barged their way past her.

Matthew stood across the street, leaning against a lamppost, hands in the pockets of the coat she'd left hanging up this morning for him to reclaim.

On seeing her, he straightened and crossed the road towards her.

Tessa's heart somersaulted. So many shifts over the past six years she'd caught herself daydreaming that she'd walk out the gates at the end of the day to find Matthew waiting for her, that he'd have come home to her for good.

'I'm glad you're home,' she told him when he arrived beside her.

'Did you bring Victoria?'

'Said I would, didn't I?' Matthew's tone was irritable as he frowned at her. 'I left her playing with Anne and Victor. She'll be all right for a bit, she's got a house full of Coopers to keep an eye on her.'

He'd know what was going on at Roddey Street, Tessa realised. Now they'd stopped keeping it all hushed up, there was no reason why they'd not be singing it from the rooftops, especially with how keen Lil was to escape Birmingham, and how excited Dorrie and Bea were to set themselves up in business together.

Matthew would feel it, too, same as Tessa did. No matter how Dorrie bent over backwards attempting to reassure them they'd no need to look for somewhere else to live, the minute she'd signed the contract on number 27, it had stopped being their home.

It was Dorrie's now, all of it, and one day it would be Bea's. The house and the shop would be kept in the Cooper family for years to come.

Not one single brick of it had ever been owned by a Lane, and now it never would be.

'We need to talk, Tess,' Matthew murmured, his expression sombre as he looked straight at her. 'There's things I need to tell you.'

Tessa nodded, slipping her arm through his. It wasn't all that long ago that he'd have reached for her hand and been holding it tightly before he'd said one word to her; as yet his hands were still buried deep in his pockets.

So he'd no desire to hold her hand then, she thought sadly. At least he hadn't objected to having her arm resting in the crook of his.

'Shall we go for a walk round the park?' she suggested.

Matthew shrugged.

'If you want.'

This end of the day they'd have no luck catching a tram out to the Lickey Hills, and the park was the next best thing, a patch of green solitude plonked in the middle of a dull, grey and broken city.

In truth she just wanted Matthew to herself for a while, and they'd take that bit longer if they took a detour around the park instead of heading straight back. And if he was ready to talk about Tom, he'd perhaps feel more like confiding in her if they weren't surrounded on all sides by brick dust and rubble.

'Got your coat back then,' Matthew noticed, as they passed through the gap between hedges, where a pair of colossal iron gates had once heralded the entrance to the park. 'Thought Bea said you'd had it pinched?'

'Turns out it was just borrowed,' Tessa told him quietly. 'By Iris Phelps,' she added, her eyes fixed on him to catch his expression.

She'd have to tell him sooner or later that she'd found the address in his pocket and took herself off to see Iris, that she knew what had happened to Tom, and now was as good a time as any.

'Borrowing without asking is stealing in my book,' he said bluntly, as though that was the only bit that mattered, as though the name Iris meant nothing to him at all. Tessa felt him tense up beside her.

'She told me about Tom,' she ventured. 'I know how you looked out for him.'

'He was my wingman for a bit,' Matthew retorted tersely. 'There were plenty before him, and there's been plenty since.' He breathed out slowly. 'You've been to see Iris, then? Thought you said you'd no idea where to look?'

He remembered, then, Tessa thought. He remembered the letter she'd written, how she'd poured out every detail of that first night Iris had emerged from the shadows of Hockley Street. She'd told him every bit of it, not least the trifling detail that it had been Iris who'd took her mother's coat, and yet Matthew had spoken as if he'd no idea where it had got to.

Perhaps he just couldn't bring up the subject of Iris Phelps, because then he'd have to talk about Tom, and what had happened to him. But he'd left her address in his pocket, he'd just left it there for Tessa to find, and hadn't he said he needed to talk to her?

'I found her address in your coat pocket, didn't I?' she reminded him. 'Course, I didn't know it was her address. Thought I was just going to look over Hilary's house, but then Iris answered the door.'

'You went through my pockets?' Matthew halted, turning to frown at her.

'Don't you trust me, Tess?'

'You left it there for me to find,' she faltered, but she wasn't as sure as she had been, not with how bitterly he was looking at her. 'Why else did you lend me your coat when I'd a perfectly decent one of my own?'

Matthew shook his head slowly, in absolute disbelief as he turned away from her.

'You were cold, Tess, so I lent you my coat. I'd not even thought what was in the pockets.'

He walked briskly ahead of her for the few paces it took him to reach the nearest bench, on to which he slumped, hunched down into his coat and avoiding her eyes as she sat down beside him.

'That's where you'd got to,' she said quietly. 'Saturday morning, when you said you were off down the bus depot. You went to see Iris instead.'

Matthew breathed out, slowly and raggedly.

'That address has been in my pocket months, Tess. I'd forgotten I even had it.'

'So where did you go?' she asked him. 'I know you went nowhere near the depot.'

'Got to account for every minute of my day now, have I?' he demanded. 'Besides, I'd no need to go to the depot, had I? Not when you were sneaking there behind my back.'

'I wasn't sneaking anywhere.' Hurt, Tessa gazed at him. 'I just wanted you to have your old job back, so we could start picking up the pieces.'

Matthew turned to look at her, a dullness in his eyes that made her feel desolate suddenly, and frightened, she wasn't quite sure why.

'Not as easy as that, Tess. You can't expect things to go back to how they were. Take more than getting back behind the wheel of a bus, that will.'

'I know,' she protested faintly. 'I know what you've been through was horrible.'

'You don't.' It was the verbal equivalent of a full stop. No room for argument.

'All lies, then, was it? Every letter you wrote?'

'Didn't tell you half of it. Not allowed to, they'd have scribbled all over it. Anyway, I didn't want to. I was trying to protect you, Tess.'

'You didn't have to do that.' Tentatively she covered his hand with hers, half expecting him to snatch it away, but for the moment he left it where it was. 'Matthew, talk to me. Please. We've always talked about everything.'

'It's not that simple.'

'Course it is.'

He might know more than she did of the horrors of flying into battle and losing comrades night after night, but she knew what it was to be one half of a marriage so solid there was nothing she'd not trust him with, and up until now she'd believed he felt the same.

Whatever he needed to talk about, it wouldn't matter how hard it was to hear. If he wanted to tell her, she wanted to listen. It was that simple.

'We're still us,' she murmured. 'There's no war can change that, Matthew.'

'But it's changed me,' he whispered.

'I'm not who I was. What I've done, Tess, you don't know me, not like you used to.'

'Day's not yet come when you're a stranger to me, Matthew Lane,' Tessa retorted fiercely, but her heart felt as though it might burst any minute, and she felt frightened again, and still she didn't know why, only that he'd something he was working up to telling her.

Something she wasn't ready to hear.

He didn't love her any more. Six years apart had been too long. Their bond had been splintered, blasted to bits in a chaos of fire and shrapnel.

'Tess . . .'

'Where did you go, Matthew?' she whispered, hearing distinctly the tremor in her own voice. 'Saturday morning, when you were out for hours, where did you go?'

'I just walked,' he said flatly. 'I was all set to go down the depot and ask after my old job, but I was halfway there and I just stopped because I couldn't for the life of me remember why it mattered.'

'You could have come home,' she

murmured. 'I told you it was a bit quick, you going off like that when you'd only been back five minutes.'

'I needed to think, Tess.'

'You had to be halfway across Brum for that, did you?'

Her voice came out all sharp and bitter. She'd not meant to sound like that, but her nerves were jumping about all over the place. How was it possible she felt more frightened now than when she'd had to worry over him flying into battle night after night?

But the war hadn't needed to take him from her, had it? Not when he'd been planning to do it himself.

'Tess, I've something to tell you.' He spoke barely above a whisper, but she heard every word as if he'd bellowed it down her ear. 'I had a letter, before I was stood down. From the commanding officer at Hawarden, offering me a post.'

'But the war's over,' Tessa protested faintly. 'You've come home.'

'Country still needs an air force,' he told her. 'And the CO at Hawarden wants me back in my old job training up the new recruits.' He looked at her. 'I called in to see him on my way to fetch Victoria.'

Tessa felt chilled to her bones.

'That's why you didn't want me going with you,' she concluded flatly, and Matthew nodded.

'I need time to think what I want, Tess.'

'So you've not accepted the post yet?' A glimmer of hope lifted her spirits a little. 'They're not expecting you back there?'

He shook his head.

'Not yet. I've some leave owing to me first, anyway. I'm to give them an answer by the end of it.'

'Be yes, won't it?' Tessa's voice trembled. 'No wonder you changed your mind about going down the depot. You'd no intention of stopping, had you? Can't get away from me fast enough.'

'Tess, you know I love you.' Matthew sighed heavily. 'No matter where I am I love you. Shouldn't have to tell you that.'

'But you're leaving me again.'

Just like that it was six years ago and she was standing at New Street station, tears spilling down her face as she watched the train pull out, Matthew's arm eventually unidentifiable amongst all the others. Half of them, perhaps more than that, wouldn't ever set foot back on Brummie soil; they'd been landed with a one-way ticket away from their loved ones.

But Matthew had been spared. He'd come back, and Tessa had been able to sleep properly again, knowing he was safe. Even if he'd not loved her any more, he'd been out of danger and that was worth the world to her.

She'd have to do it all again now, over and over, every time he went back after his leave. Even when the war was properly over and done with, she'd worry. As long as Matthew worked on a military base he'd be a target.

What if there were more wars in future? He'd be in the thick of it all over again, and she'd never rest easy.

The war had taken him from her after all.

Victory in Japan

At a pace so brisk her feet were nearly taking flight beneath her, Tessa hurtled back along Hockley Street.

It was Lil and Bertie's last night. This time tomorrow they'd be sitting down to dinner with Granny Peg. Miles away they'd be; no matter how Lil kept going on about how easy it would be to visit. Guilty conscience, that was; Lil knew she'd stitched Tessa up good and proper, talking her into starting up in business together and then selling up once Tessa's talent had earned Lil a nice little nest egg.

Bit more to it than that, Tessa reminded herself. Lil hadn't been happy, and now she was all smiles, looking forward to bringing up her children in a peaceful Welsh valley. Back in the cottage where she and her ma had sat at Peg's piano and sung their hearts out. Lil's heart needed to mend, and it'd take more than a needle and thread to do that.

Still a little way off, Tessa found her feet slowing of their own accord as she watched Victoria carefully wheeling Victor's pram out of the shop, Anne at her side as she so often was now Victoria had finished school for the summer.

It had done her good, Tessa mused, having Anne and Victor to help look after. She doted on the pair of them, Victoria did. She'd miss them when they went. Not all one-sided, either. Anne adored Victoria; she was her big sister, best friend and fairy-tale princess all rolled into one.

'Where are you three off to at this hour?' Tessa asked, as the girls rolled Victor's pram towards her.

'Walking Victor to sleep,' Anne informed her.

'Keeping these two out from under their feet, aren't I?' Victoria added, nodding her head back towards the house. 'Last-minute packing, there's boxes all over the place. Lil's got herself in a right lather.'

She reached over the side of the pram

to kiss Victor's rosy cheek, and he chuckled as he grasped her finger.

'Granny Peg will have a house full by this time tomorrow,' Victoria commented flatly. 'No wonder she wanted me out the way.'

'Wasn't like that, was it?' Tessa corrected her. 'You're back here because it's your home.'

'Except I'm in the way here, too,' Victoria said bitterly. 'I'd been back in Brum five minutes and Uncle Matthew was dumping me on Lil so you two could go off on your own for a bit.' She sighed. 'Don't blame you, though. I'm not your daughter, am I?'

'Victoria, that's not how it was,' Tessa began, but Victoria turned back to Anne, painting on a smile when she glimpsed the alarm in the little girl's bright green eyes.

'Right then, Anne, we'd best take this chap for a stroll, hadn't we? He'll be waking the whole street up, else.'

Tessa stood a minute, watching them trundle off along the pavement.

If Victoria only knew, she thought bitterly, it'd just be the two of them soon enough. Matthew hadn't said for definite he'd be going back to Hawarden, but he'd done nothing about getting his old job back at the depot either. When he'd not turned up, Alf Piatt had made a house call, dropping by to remind Matthew he was keeping a spot open for him.

'Being headhunted for a decent job, he is, when there's thousands like him coming back to no means of putting a crust of bread on the table,' Bea had grumbled when Tessa had confided in her. 'Mind you, air force is what he knows now, Tess. Suppose it makes more sense than a life he can barely remember.'

But she'd been part of that life, Tessa thought sadly, the most important part. So why not just pack up the dregs of her life and catch the next train to Wales? She could find a house to rent close by Hawarden so she'd see more of Matthew, and Victoria could return to a life of fields and animals and muddy gumboots.

Perhaps that's what she should do then. Start again from scratch, and just be thankful she could.

'Getting a bit nippy out there now, Tess,' Bea commented that evening, when they were sitting sharing a pot of tea. 'Good job you've got your ma's coat back to keep the frost off you.'

'Reckon that would have been the last you'd seen of it if you'd not tracked down that Iris Phelps,' Lil chipped in. 'Weren't falling over herself to bring it back, was she?'

You'd be forgiven for thinking Lil and Bea were old friends these days, Tessa thought, hiding a smile. Since Dorrie had stumped up the money to change both their lives for the better, Lil had stopped envying Bea her close relationship with her mother and Bea had stopped feeling pushed out with Tessa and the shop. The pair of them were as thick as thieves all of a sudden.

'Our Anne's out like a light,' Dorrie announced, bustling into the room. 'Bertie and Matthew took themselves off down the Black Horse, have they?'

'One last pint before I drag him off to Wales.' Lil grinned, passing the cakes. 'Thanks, Dorrie. Here, have one of your cakes.'

'Don't mind if I do. As it's a special occasion, like.' Dorrie took a cake and settled back against the cushions to eat it. 'Victoria not joining us, Tess?'

'Got her nose in a book,' Tessa told her. 'She'll be reading 'til all hours.'

'She'll miss my two, won't she?' Lil acknowledged. 'Been a treasure with them these past weeks, she has.' She looked at Tessa pointedly. 'Still, there's nothing stopping the lot of you coming to visit, is there?'

'You're not the only one moving,' Tessa said quickly, changing the subject. 'Iris Phelps is moving her and Tommy in with her parents.'

'About time if you ask me!' Dorrie exclaimed. 'Not right, a young girl like that too proud to ask her own parents for a bit of help when she needs it.'

'She said they were that chuffed to see

her, and little Tommy,' Tessa reflected. 'All bad feeling went out the window, by the sounds of it.'

'And where's that leave Hilary's house?' Lil queried.

'Way things are round here, it'll not be empty for long, will it?' Bea reasoned. 'Corporation will have that house occupied before Iris has her feet properly out the door.'

Lil shook her head sadly.

'Tell you what else isn't right, strangers living in Hilary's house.' She hesitated, looking straight at Tessa. 'Not when you could take it, you and Matthew, and Victoria.'

'With what?' Tessa sighed. 'I'd need a deposit, and I've not got that sort of money rattling around.'

'Tess?' Dorrie's voice broke into her thoughts. 'You've more than enough to pay a deposit, and the first six months' rent at least, I reckon.'

Tessa stared at her blankly.

'I haven't,' she began, but Bea interrupted her.

'Your share of the profits from this place, Tess.'

'My share?' she echoed. 'I'm not entitled to a penny of it. The profits are yours, not mine.'

'Without you we'd have no profits, Tess,' Dorrie reminded her. 'It's your creations folk clamour for, your name over that door. If we're doing well now it's only because you've made us a household name hereabouts.'

They wanted her out, Tessa realised. Once Lil and Bertie took the children tomorrow, Dorrie and Bea would be halfway to having the house to themselves. Perhaps it was worth parting with a chunk of the shop's profits if it meant Tessa and her family would be out from under their feet.

'Reckon it'd mean a lot to Matthew if you were to set up home together in his sister's house,' Lil told her, but Tessa shook her head, unable to stop her voice dripping bitterness. 'Make no difference to him where we live if he's not here, will it?'

* * *

The clock on the mantel had just chimed midnight when Matthew and Bertie burst in the door. Dorrie muttered as she leapt up to check the children hadn't been disturbed, but Bertie grabbed her arm as she bustled past him.

'No, Ma, wait. Listen.'

Matthew had gone straight to the wireless and he was fiddling with it, all fingers and thumbs as he tuned the knob to the right frequency.

Silence settled over the lot of them, Tessa noted; the whole room waiting as one and hardly daring to hope. Then the wireless stopped crackling and the Prime Minister made the announcement the world had been waiting for. Victory over Japan, and the end of World War II. It was all over.

* * *

How long had it been since they'd sat side by side on the doorstep, looking up at the stars together? Everyone else had gone up to bed now, there was just Tessa and Matthew, sitting on the top step outside Li'l Tessa's, watching the world go by, like they used to.

There were folk milling about in the street, dancing and singing with joy and relief. Nothing like the scale of festivities they'd seen on VE night, but it had been late when the announcement had been broadcast. No doubt tomorrow would see more than its fair share of merriment. 'Are you cold, Tess?' Matthew murmured, and she shook her head.

'Not cold. Are you?'

'Not any more' He reached an arm around her and she nestled into his shoulder. 'It's over. I can't believe it's over.'

'And I've still got you,' Tessa whispered, and she turned her face to kiss him. 'I love you, Matthew Lane.'

It almost didn't matter that he might go off again and leave her, that the air force might reclaim him. It would matter in the morning, she thought. For now all that mattered was that he was here, beside her, and he was safe.

They both were. They'd made it through the war and they'd landed back here, gazing up at the stars.

'I love you, too, Tess,' he said softly. 'With all my heart.'

'I know.' She reached for his hand and held it tight. 'You and me — like always.'

Matthew was quiet for a minute, holding her close to him. He turned to kiss the top of Tessa's head.

'My Tess,' he whispered. 'I'm so sorry.'

'For what? You've nothing to be sorry for.'

Matthew exhaled heavily.

'I need to tell you. And I can't . . .' he swallowed '. . . I can't carry this on my own.'

'You don't need to.' Tessa lifted her head and looked straight into his hazel eyes, her own filling with tears. 'You tell me everything, do you hear?'

He sighed raggedly, and began to speak.

'On the base we called him Taffy.

Welsh for friend, see.'

'Tom Phelps?' Tessa prompted quietly, and he nodded, and then it came out in a rush. As if now he'd started, he had to get the words out quick, before they got so hard and painful he'd never be rid of them.

'He had combat fatigue, we all did. Flying out day after day, night after night, it gets to feel like that's all there is, and that's all you want there to be, because if you stop to remember what else there is, knowing you might lose everything, it's too hard to bear, Tess.'

He hesitated, taking a breath to steady himself before he went on. Tessa raised his hand to her mouth and kissed it.

'I knew Tom was at the end of the line,' he confessed, and his voice trembled. 'He was exhausted, losing concentration all over the place. So I spoke to the CO and he swung it for Tom to be taken off active service. They were sending him to instruct. His posting came through, it was all sorted. Thing is, while I was reading it, safe in my nice little office, he was up in a Spit, getting blown to bits.'

'His posting came through too late,' Tessa murmured, and Matthew swallowed hard.

'Too late,' he echoed. 'I'd left it too long to speak to the CO. I wrote to Iris. I wanted to be the one to tell her, and I said you'd help her. I didn't know what else I could do.'

'It's all right,' Tessa told him, but he shook his head.

'No. I'd no right, not after not coming back to see you on VE Day. I knew I'd hurt you, Tess. But it was easier just to shut out emotion. I knew if I came back and saw you, I'd not be able to leave again.' His eyes were brimming with tears as he gazed at her. 'But if I go back now, if I take this post at Hawarden, and I train up the next Taffy, and the next, I can make amends for losing Tom.'

She'd not tell him he didn't need to. She'd just put her arms around him and hold him tight, and she'd tell him what he needed her to say.

'Go to Hawarden, Matthew. It'll be all

right, I promise.'

Next morning she knew, as soon as she opened her eyes. He'd gone.

She'd her own life to be getting on with anyway; his, too, when he came back on leave to be with them for a bit. She'd take her share of the profits from Li'l Tessa's and pay the deposit on Hilary's house. Whatever it took to jump the queue, she'd do it, because Victoria deserved to live in the house her mum had wanted for her. They'd fetch Hazel and Scrapes back from Granny Peg's, she promised Victoria, they'd have a grand time tearing about the garden.

'You still want me then,' Victoria faltered. 'With Uncle Matthew gone off again, you've no reason to keep a roof over my head.'

'Course I have. Best reason in the world.' Tessa put her arms around her and Victoria relaxed into her shoulder. 'I love you, don't I?' Her mind at rest, Victoria ran to her room, to write a letter to her gran about fetching the cats.

Tessa wandered outside into the street.

She wanted to have a minute to herself before she went back in to join Lil and the rest. And there he was, plain as day, her Matthew. Walking back along Hockley Street, towards her, and when he got there, he took her hand and placed something cold into the palm, closing her fingers securely over it.

'The key to Hilary's house,' he told her. 'Our house. I paid the deposit with the last of my pay from the RAF. My very last pay,' he added, drawing her close to him and whispering the words she'd waited so long to hear. 'I'm not going back, Tess. I didn't even know it until you told me to go, then I realised that's exactly why I couldn't.' He rested his forehead against hers. 'You're so brave and selfless, I know you didn't want me to go, but you'd have said nothing and let me leave.'

'I thought you had,' Tessa whispered.

'I'm going nowhere,' he said fiercely. 'I promise you that. You and me, remember?'

She nodded, tears of joy spilling down

her cheeks, as he kissed her.

'I love you, Tessa. But there's something I need to ask you.' He smiled at her, lifting her hand to his mouth to kiss her wedding band. 'Will you marry me . . . again?'

It was a good job they'd decided against waiting for all the VJ Day celebrations to fizzle out first, Tessa thought. The country was having a right old knees-up, they'd have been waiting for ever. Jeannie had been good enough to close the Black Horse to the public just for one afternoon, so Tessa and Matthew could celebrate renewing their vows.

Bea and Victoria were maids of honour, Victoria thrilled to bits because Granny Peg had travelled down with Lil and Bertie, the icing on the cake being that she'd persuaded Hazel and Scrapes into a travelling basket, so they were now settling into their new home on Belgrave Road and no doubt causing a bit of mischief to the living-room curtains.

Anne was her flower girl, and Mary, too, of course, and even Victor looked smart in a little baby suit. Iris had brought Tommy along, and the pair of them looked happy.

Course, Bertie couldn't resist taking to the piano, to belt out a few merry tunes. For today at least the world was back to how it should be, Tessa thought happily, resting her head on Matthew's shoulder as Lil, resplendent in the emerald brooch her daughter had saved up to buy her, took her place at Bertie's side once more, and sang like an angel.